P9-COP-063

TWELVE
LONG
MONTHS

BRIAN MALLOY

Scholastic Press ❖ New York

Library of Congress Cataloging-in-Publication Data

Mallory, Brian.
    Twelve long Months / Brian Malloy. — 1st ed.
        p. cm.
    "Levithan /Scholastic Press."
    Summary: From the end of her senior year at Minnesota's Le Sueur High School through her first year as a physics major at Columbia University, Molly Swain finds the inner strength and good friends to help her cope with huge challenges, including learning that the boy she loves is gay.
    ISBN-13: 978-0-439-87761-9 (hardcover : alk. paper)
    ISBN-10: 0-439-87761-X (hardcover : alk. paper)
    [1. Self-actualization (Psychology)—Fiction.   2. Interpersonal relations—Fiction.
3. Homosexuality—Fiction.   4. College freshmen—Fiction.   5. Columbia
University—Fiction.   6. New York (N.Y.)—Fiction.   7. Minnesota—Fiction.]   I. Title.
    PZ7.M2954Twe 2008
    [Fic] —dc22

                                                            2007043370

10 9 8 7 6 5 4 3 2 1   08 09 10 11 12 13

Printed in the U.S.A.   23
First edition, June 2008

Book design by Alison Klapthor

This book is for my mother and my fathers, and for Terry.

For his faith in the idea, help with the drafts, and encouragement along the way, special thanks to David Levithan. Thanks, too, to Julie Schumacher, Charles Baxter, Anne Ursu, and Meigan Rath for their valuable input and feedback.

As we fix our sight on the future and anticipate all the wonders yet in store for us, we should also reflect back and marvel at the journey we have taken so far.

— from *The Elegant Universe* by Brian Greene

MAY

I cannot fathom why I am in love with Mark Dahl.

It's all I can do not to reach out and touch him, not to place a hand on his cheek. Not to run my fingers through his dark brown — nearly black — hair, not to hold him tight and never let go. I wonder what it would feel like, his arms around me, his lips pressed against mine. I imagine our breathing as our tongues dance together, perhaps a sigh here or there as he strokes my hair.

I hug myself as I try to picture it, but picturing it is hard to do since I've never really kissed a boy. This unfortunate little fact makes me sad, so I squeeze myself a little tighter.

He strolls into chemistry class late (as usual), barely picking up his feet. His sneakers make a soft shushing sound as he walks. He sees me and asks, "You cold?"

I put my arms back at my sides, grin (too broadly, not attractive, stupid, stupid, stupid), and shake my head because I find it hard to speak when he's around. I'm afraid of what I might say — things like *I love you* and *You're so cute.* I've worn some makeup today, nothing over the top, just some foundation to even out my white and blotchy skin tone.

Mark is my lab partner. We didn't choose each other; our teacher, Mr. Sanchez, paired us off nearly eight months ago. *Swain, Molly, and Dahl, Mark.* Now Mark hands me a notebook, my notebook, the one I gave him so he could copy my work. He's probably going to get an A in chemistry, his first A ever. Because I let him copy everything. Because I've never once leaned over a test to hide my answers from his prying eyes; if anything, I've nearly killed my back, perching awkwardly atop my stool to give him the best possible view of my answers. Back in November, Mr. Sanchez said, *Why, Molly, you must be a good influence on Mark. He's getting perfect scores.* He'd smirked when he said it, perhaps warning me not to let Mark's clear skin and sleepy smile get the best of me.

Mark.

Tall, skinny Mark with the thin lips and the eyes like he just woke up.

Mark says thanks, and I stare at my notebook, the one I will save forever, because it's the only thing we've ever shared. Mark has carried it in his hands, perhaps flipping through the pages as he lay down on a couch, staring at my handwriting, trying to make sense of it.

I nod, as if to say, "No problem." I open the notebook to look for any new drawings he may have added since last time. Mark's an artist, and sometimes my notebook gets to be his canvas.

We sit on our stools and lean on the counter, the one with sinks in it. At the other end, sitting next to a different sink, is Donna Piambino, who has made significant parts of my life hell for the last four years, and her lab partner, a football player who shaves his head bald. Donna notices me. She gives me a nasty look and I turn away.

Mr. Sanchez, who stands at the front of the classroom, folds his arms over his little potbelly and asks, "You know what you're supposed to be doing, so why am I waiting?"

Mark watches as I set up our beakers and burners. I measure and pour as Mark stifles a yawn. Finally, he asks, "You want me to take notes?"

I smile, say, "No, thanks, I can take care of it."

He grins lazily with those thin lips and says, "You know, you're the only reason I'm gonna get an A in this class."

I smile again, letting my hair fall over my face

because I know I'm blushing, *really* blushing, the kind of bright red glow that only gets worse when I try to make it stop. Every day, and I mean EVERY DAY, I tell myself that if Mark were fat and ugly I would never have helped him. Next, I always tell myself that I am shallow, that I have acted against my own better judgment just because I like looking at him, that I have taken my integrity — which used to be *really important* to me — and shoved it away somewhere. But I can't help myself. True, he doesn't say much, except *'Sup?* And, yes, when he does address me directly, he often calls me *Dude*, but I know that beneath these simpleminded catchphrases is a deep and complicated boy who understands that life is not predicable, like classical physics would have us believe, but merely a series of probabilities, as quantum mechanics teaches us.

Mark runs a hand through his hair — his marvelous, thick hair — and sighs.

I ask, "Rough night?"

He nods drowsily. Mark's a farm kid, not a town kid, and it seems all he ever does is work: milking cows, baling hay, plowing fields. This past spring when the calves were born, he didn't sleep at all for days.

While I've always sort of liked Mark, it wasn't until

back in February that I really fell hard for him. Even though it was around Valentine's Day, I wasn't influenced by cheap sentiment like cards and candy and flowers. I've never gotten any anyway (except from my parents, which doesn't count), so I wasn't missing what I'd never had.

When he walked into class that dark, snowy day in February, I noticed his eyes were glassy and I assumed he had gotten high with some of his friends. He was wearing a threadbare gray sweater that smelled like hay and his jeans were dirty at the knees. I could tell that he hadn't washed his hair; it looked stiff and one side seemed plastered to his head.

Mr. Sanchez stopped his lecture and said, "Mark, why do you even bother showing up at all?"

Mark nodded a little, as if Mr. Sanchez had just said, "Good afternoon."

I smiled at Mark and continued my work. But then I stopped, surprised to see that somehow Mark had managed to balance himself on the stool and fall sound asleep, with his head resting on his arms on the countertop. I looked down at his closed eyes, at the strand of dirty hair that covered an eye. I could hear the little inhalations and exhalations, and all I wanted was to hold him in my arms as he slept. He looked handsome and vulnerable. My heart melted when he sighed slightly.

When he woke himself up with a little snort after only a few minutes, he looked around, embarrassed.

I said, "You're lucky Mr. Sanchez didn't catch you."

He just rubbed his eyes and, smiling, whispered, "Sorry, Molly."

And I smiled and shook my head, disapproving not of him but of myself. I thought about all the reasons he could never fall for someone like me, and why I should not fall for someone like him.

But it didn't matter, because at that precise moment in time I realized it was too late.

I look at him now, feigning interest in our experiment.

I write a bit in my notebook, jotting down quantities and observations. In the margins Mark has drawn one of his superhero characters. And so it goes, me mixing and measuring and scribbling down notes, and Mark doodling pictures of dogs in capes and musclemen in skintight costumes clenching their fists, deciding between flight or fight.

While I enjoy chemistry, my absolute favorite is physics, in particular, quantum mechanics, which they do not teach at Le Sueur High but which I study on my own. In quantum mechanics, everything is based on probability. For example, if you try to walk through a wall, you will *probably* fail, but not *certainly* fail. In his book *The Elegant Universe*, Brian Greene, a physicist who teaches at Columbia (where I'm going to college in the fall), writes that quantum mechanics . . . *shows that if you walked into a solid wall every second, you would have to wait longer than the current age of the universe to have a good chance of passing through it on one of your attempts. With eternal patience (and longevity), though, you could — sooner or later — emerge on the other side.* This gives me some small bit of hope that I can change what is probable (Mark continues to fail to recognize that I exist in any real sense of the word) to what is possible (Mark falls madly, passionately, and deeply in love with me).

I am a fool for possibilities.

For the past few days I've been heading straight home from school, not stopping by the new library to use the computers or the Super America for a candy bar (I really *have* to lose at least ten pounds — when I move to New York in the fall I want to look amazing . . . well, amazing for me). When I arrive at the tiny house I call home, I have the place to myself. Mom is at her shift at Boss Burger and Dad's probably somewhere in Pennsylvania right now. Dad's a trucker and hates driving through Pennsylvania because of the Pennsylvania Turnpike, which he says is "highway robbery, literally, highway robbery! And the lanes are so goddamned narrow!" I hope he's keeping his promise to cut down on the Big Macs and Whoppers and supersize fries and shakes. He's got these really muscular arms and broad shoulders, but his stomach makes him look like he's in his third trimester.

I wander through the crowded little living room, with its mismatched furniture. I always cringe at the bent floral couch that sits next to the faded plaid recliner that my dad found sitting on a curb, waiting for the garbagemen. I enter the small kitchen with its pressed-wood cabinets and warped linoleum floor — not exactly out of *Better Homes and Gardens.* There, on the messy table, are the breakfast dishes waiting for me to wash them and put them away.

They can wait a few minutes. I grab a bag of ridged potato chips — five or six won't be too awful — and crunch away. When I try to take my mind off Mark, I think about Brian Greene. He's the major reason I applied to Columbia. I was first introduced to him via a *NOVA* series called *The Elegant Universe*, which was based on his book of the same name. I thought he made quantum physics really accessible for the average person (or even the below-average person, like my brother, not that he would ever watch *NOVA*), and I liked his smile, which seemed very sincere. He was passionate about helping viewers understand superstring theory, which seeks to explain the universe and everything in it in a single, unified theory. There are some parents at my school who think we shouldn't be taught alternative theories of the universe or even evolution; they think existence begins and ends with God. And we have a lot of self-proclaimed Christian students at Le Sueur High, but they tend to fall into two groups: 1) the ones who think they're rebels because the liberal media controls the country, and 2) the ones who say they're Christian but still do drugs and have sex like everybody except me.

Anyway, Brian Greene, whom I admire, is too old for me, but I do hope to meet a younger version of him one day, someone who is truly inquisitive about the universe and our place in it; someone who seeks to discover a unified theory for everything, including us.

If only that person could be Mark Dahl.

I'm suddenly aware of my brother, Russ, a fifteen-year-old *dude* who always seems to appear out of nowhere when I want some time to myself. Russ leans against the noisy, ancient refrigerator, his long brown hair flowing over his shoulders. He says, "'Sup, Molly-Pop?"

"Don't call me that."

He smirks. "Gotta get it in while I can. When you move to New York I'll have to buy a phone card to give you shit."

A bit of potato chip slips out of my mouth as I tell him, "I'm getting an unlisted number."

He one-ups me: "Aren't you on a diet?"

I swallow hard. "I can eat whatever I want; it's all about moderation and exercise."

"O for two, Molly-Pop."

"Shouldn't you be out with your loser friends?"

He heads out of the kitchen as he says, "Just leaving, don't freak out." He pauses at the potato chips and grabs a handful for himself. "There's a message for you from the scholarship lady. They want a black-and-white head shot of you."

I think about my high school graduation picture, which is in color and makes me look fat. "Okay."

"It has to be digital, too. She said it's going to be in their annual report."

Once I hear the front door slam shut behind him, I grab the bag of chips. The scholarship is from the Rural Women's Society. One of their goals is to get girls from the sticks like me a college education in a traditionally male field — in my case, physics. There are two other winners this year from Minnesota: a Mexican-American girl from Thief River Falls who's going to study marine biology and a fifty-year-old "displaced housewife" from Granite Falls who's going to be an auto mechanic. I met them in Minneapolis when the Society hosted a brunch for this year's winners and gave us these oversized checks that they had us pose with. The picture made the front page of the *Le Sueur News Herald*.

It was really embarrassing because I'm smiling with my eyes closed.

And if that wasn't bad enough, Russ made a huge copy of the photo, replacing the background with a high-way scene and the check I was holding with a sign that said NEED RIDE TO *STAR TREK* CONVENTION.

When Mark joins me at our counter for fifth-period chemistry the next day, I smile at the sight of him (too broadly, not attractive, stupid, stupid, stupid) and say, "How're you doing?"

Mark looks at me and I notice stubble on his chin and under his nose.

It's just *too* adorable.

"I'm cool," he says matter-of-factly as he hands me my notebook.

In about three months I will be in New York and Mark will still be in Minnesota. Just the thought of it makes me want to cry. Mom and Dad are pressuring me to use the scholarship to go somewhere locally. Just the idea of New York scares them, so I haven't told them yet that I've already enrolled at Columbia.

In my notebook Mark has drawn a new character, Mad Cow, the World's Angriest Bovine. It's basically a *Hulk* rip-off — when the cow gets mad it morphs into this muscle-bound freak of nature and levels slaughter-houses. Still, it's cute in a bizarre sort of way. I notice Mad Cow is atop the Empire State Building like King Kong, trying to knock biplanes out of the air.

I look at him, a little grin on his thin lips. I ask, "Mad Cow has moved to New York?"

Mark looks at me now, really looks at me, and

smiles. "Mad Cow has to. I'm heading east. We'll be neighbors."

"You're *kidding* me!"

"I've got an uncle in New Jersey who paints houses. I'm going to work for him. That is, if I graduate. That's the deal."

"Where in New Jersey?" I ask, too urgently, like my life depended on knowing.

"Montclair."

As soon as I get home I'm looking up Montclair on the Web. New Jersey is right next door to New York, so Montclair can't be too far from Manhattan. Please God, if you exist, don't let Montclair be too far from Manhattan.

This is the universe sending me a signal that maybe, *just maybe*, Mark and I will end up together.

He continues, "We'll have to hang out in the city sometime. I've never been to New York."

I nod, not trusting my voice, which I think would squeal. I try to think of something, anything, to say.

I've gotten my foot through the wall.

Maybe when he comes to visit me in Manhattan we'll see a Broadway show and then go out for a late dinner in Little Italy. Maybe he'll leave New Jersey behind and stay on in New York. Maybe we'll get married and settle down in the city that never sleeps and send our kids to a private academy where it is their intellect that is admired rather than their good looks or outstanding athletic ability. And *unlike* at Le Sueur High School, no one would feel like a big loser if they didn't have a date for the senior prom.

I look at Mark, his shaggy hair hanging in front of his face. I risk speaking.

"It'll be fun to hang out in New York!" I say.

He nods. "It'll be good to know someone out there."

For the first time since the Rural Women called with the news about the scholarship, I'm feeling joy. But then I have to open my mouth.

For some reason, I say, "I wonder who you're taking to the prom."

Oh. Dear. God.

I *think* that came out of me. I look around to be sure.

Mark looks up from the Bunsen burner. He shakes the hair out of his eyes, blinks a bit. He mumbles, "The prom's not till next week."

"Not much time to find a date." I should get my lips sewn shut. That way I wouldn't be physically able to say stupid things and I'd finally lose ten pounds.

Mark grunts. "Are *you* gonna go?"

I shrug, make a little *pfffft* sound with my tongue and lips. "No." I might as well add, *Of course not.*

He stares into the flame now, like a cat. "I'm not going to the prom . . . it's such a waste of money. Besides, if you don't have to go, why do I?"

Because any girl in her right mind would go with you in a nanosecond, maybe less. Well, that's not entirely true. Just the shallow ones, like me.

"No reason," I say. "Sorry."

He looks like he's just come out of a trance, the kind the hypnotist puts you in before they tell you to squawk like a chicken. I saw it happen once on a talk show when I was just a kid.

"It's cool," he says.

And here I am, opening my mouth again, and this time I hear myself say, "It's just weird; you could take anyone you wanted."

He mutters as he shakes his head. "Yeah, *right.*" After a second he asks, "So why aren't you going?"

I sigh. "Because no one asked me." Then I quickly add, "Let me change my answer: Because no one *will* ask me."

He runs a finger through the flame, too quickly to burn his skin. "That's all somebody has to do, ask you? If a serial murderer asked you to prom, you'd say yes?"

I frown. *"No.* I'm not *desperate,* you know." But let's face it, I am. "It's too bad, you not going. I mean, if money's a problem, I've saved some." *Stop talking, Molly! Stop talking now!* "I could loan you some so you could go."

He looks at me strangely. "Uh, Molly . . . I'm seeing someone. She goes to Mankato West."

Of course he's seeing someone.

I feel fat.

I feel empty.

Quietly, I ask him, "Really? What's her name?"

He looks at me for a second or two before he says, "Julie."

Great. I know a Julie at Mankato West. She's beautiful. I decide to punish myself some more. "Is it Julie Park?"

"No, it's Julie . . . Why do you want to know her last name?"

I whisper, "I thought I might know her. I have a cousin who goes to Mankato West."

"You don't know her."

"So you're taking Julie to the prom?"

He frowns. "No! Jeez, I told you — it's such a waste of money. Renting a tux and all that shit. We're just going out, the two of us, you know." He pauses a moment before he adds, "We're gonna have a picnic dinner by Lake Volney."

His words hit me head-on, the kind of accident that Dad occasionally passes on his trips, the ones that make him offer a prayer for travelers. I try to catch my breath. I feel like I could cry.

Mark says real loud, "Hey, Mr. Sanchez, I gotta go to the can."

Mr. Sanchez, who is helping a cheerleader clean up the counter she's spilled on, says, "Yes, Mark, you *may* go to the men's room."

Mark leaves in a hurry. From her end of the counter, Donna Piambino says, so everyone near us can hear, "Nice one, Swain."

"What's that supposed to mean?" I ask.

She scowls. "He's *so* out of your league."

Nobody says anything. I look at the next counter over, and even the captain of the cheerleading squad, the one who congratulated me on my scholarship, just stares at her beakers. I say, my voice wavering, "I don't have a crush on Mark."

Donna laughs. "A 'crush'? What are you, twelve? You get good grades, Swain, but you know shit about the real world. He wouldn't hook up with you if you were the last girl on earth."

A couple of students laugh, but then Mr. Sanchez wants to know what's so funny. I just look at the sink.

After Mark comes back, we don't say a word to each other for the rest of the class, and when the bell rings, he practically runs out of the room.

I'm such a loser.

When I get home, I find Mom there, sick with a cold, which she always blames on the kids who hang out at Boss Burger. I make her some tea and wish she would do something about her hair, which is really too long for a woman her age, and getting grayer all the time.

When I hand her a mug she says, "I'm so glad you're not down at Boss Burger every day like some of the kids from your school. You think they'd find something better to do with their time."

This is Mom's way of trying to make me feel superior for having no social life. My lifelong best friend, Maddie, moved to the Twin Cities last year after her family's farm failed. Mom takes a sip of her tea and notices the funk I'm in. She asks, "Hard day at school?"

I shrug.

She says, "Don't let it get you down. Not much longer till graduation. You know, I was talking to one of the gals at Boss Burger the other day and she told me her nephew loves the U."

I grunt, in no mood to discuss the University of Minnesota. I could tell her I've already enrolled at Columbia, but this is a battle I don't want to fight just now. So instead I tell her, "I have homework to do."

The night of the prom finds me alone in my room, trying not to think about Lake Volney, where Mark and his girlfriend from West Mankato are probably feeding each other chocolate cake with vanilla ice cream before going off into the woods to make mad, passionate love. I can't get my mind off it – Mark with his shirt unbuttoned, his girlfriend's hands running through his hair, his own hands around her waist as they tentatively make their way farther south. . . .

I open a book, one I've read about fourteen times before, *The Fabric of the Cosmos* by Brian Greene. But even a unified theory of existence can't seem to distract me; I can see Mark sketching a portrait of his girlfriend — *Julie* — as the sun sets. Or maybe the two of them, under the tall pines, are looking around to make sure no one is watching as they roll on top of each other, breathless.

Stop it.

I need a MAJOR distraction, so I walk down Main to the DVD rental place for something that will temporarily rid me of Mark Dahl, the boy I love, who, no doubt, is loving someone else while the rest of our class are dancing to a live band and making memories of their own. I make a list of what my high school memories will be:

1. Studying.
2. Loving Mark Dahl.
3. Avoiding Donna Piambino.
4. Loving Mark Dahl.
5. Avoiding the lunchroom.
6. Loving Mark Dahl.
7. Reading quantum physics in an effort to make sense out of the universe.
8. Loving Mark.

As much as I hate to admit it, maybe Donna Piambino is right. For someone who gets such good grades, I can be such a fool. I really need to watch a film about someone who is even more pathetic than I am.

Mr. Bachman, the owner of the DVD rental place, smiles at me as I enter his little shop. He says, "Hey-ya there, Molly. What ya looking for tonight? We got some new action pictures in this week."

"No, thanks. Any new tearjerkers?"

He laughs, shaking his head as he leans against his counter. "Why is it all gals love a good cry?" The monitor above him plays *Spider-Man 3*. Peter Parker and M.J. are kissing because that's what people do, even superheroes.

"I don't know," I tell him and slip down the drama aisle, searching for something set in the past. Contemporary tragedy feels too close to home.

And that's when I see him.

Mark's back is toward me, his shoulders stooped, like he's a shoplifter. I'd recognize him anywhere.

"Mark?" I ask tentatively.

He turns to face me, like he's surrendering to the police. He mutters, "Hey, Molly."

"I thought you were going to Lake Volney tonight."

"Lake Volney?"

"With Julie."

He blushes, something he rarely does. "Oh, yeah. It's a long story."

"Oh," I say. He looks sad. I'm thrilled. Maybe she dumped him. Maybe he's on the rebound. Maybe he needs someone to comfort him. Maybe that's why we both ended up here tonight.

"Whatcha doing?" he asks.

I smile, shrug. "I left the prom early. All the guys were fighting over me and it was just too embarrassing. Seems to happen wherever I go. So I thought, maybe a quiet evening in would be nice for a change. One does get tired of parties and romance."

He looks at me, a little smirk on his face. "One does."

So we stand there, looking around and occasionally at each other. After a moment or two he flicks the hair out of his eyes and says, "Well, guess I better head out."

I have to stop him. This is destiny; it cannot be toyed with. I look at his empty hands, the ones I had imagined were exploring Julie's body. I say, "But you haven't picked out a movie yet."

He thinks a moment before he says, "Why don't you pick one out? No chick flicks, though."

I *think* he just asked me out.

Did he just ask me out?

I think he just asked me out.

I say, with a little tremble in my voice, "How about a superhero movie?" Mark loves superheroes and I love Mark.

He nods. "Cool."

I say, "I can make us some popcorn."

He says "Cool" again. And it sounds worthy of Shakespeare.

Mark drives us to my house in his dad's pickup truck. I try to think of interesting, witty things to say, but I come up empty. When we arrive he plops down on one end of the couch, in front of the set, and I pop in the DVD so fast I think I may have broken it. Then I just stand there, wondering where I should sit: on the couch or on my dad's La-Z-Boy? I take so long trying to make up my mind that Mark finally says, "You forget something?"

I say "Popcorn" and rush into the kitchen. When I come back, Mark is watching the special features. I sit down next to him on the couch so we can share the bowl. Sitting next to him on our couch — it's just . . . surreal.

We're watching *Spider-Man 3* in silence and eating popcorn when Mom gets home. She's still wearing her uniform, which is embarrassing. When she sees Mark and me on the couch, she practically drops dead.

"Well, hell-low," she says, a sly look on her otherwise exhausted face. I don't pause the film, hoping she'll take the hint.

Mark stands, offers Mom his hand. "Hi, Mrs. Swain. I'm Mark."

Mom frowns, but then smiles waaay too big. "Mark Dahl *the lab partner?*"

Oh dear God.

Mark says, "Uh, yeah, I'm Molly's lab partner."

"You're the artist? The one who does Mad Cow, the World's Angriest Bovine?"

Mark laughs and says, "Yeah, that's me."

Mom looks at me. "Molly loves your drawings. She says you have real talent."

Now Mark looks at me, a little surprised. I don't move, I don't say anything; it's like I was embalmed in the sitting position.

Mom looks at the television now, asks what we're watching. When Mark tells her, she says, "Oh, I love Spider-Man." Next she sings, *"Spider-Man, Spider-Man, does whatever a spider can."*

Finally, I can speak. "Mom!"

She gives me a little look and then says, "Well, you two enjoy your movie. I'm heading upstairs for a hot shower and bed."

Once the movie ends and the credits roll, I wonder what to do next. How do I make him fall in love with me? Fate delivered him, but the rest is up to me.

He cracks an unpopped kernel between his teeth. "I think it'd be cool to have a secret identity. You know, you could live, like, two lives. The one everyone expects you to live and then this other one, where you did what you wanted."

I look at his profile, still staring at the little screen. I say, "What would your superhero name be?"

He smiles and it looks sad. "I dunno. Not even a superhero, I guess. Just who I wanted to be, you know."

I turn off the set and face him at his end of the couch, where a pillow sits on his lap like armor. "I don't understand."

He looks at me now, hugs the pillow. "My parents want me to take over the farm. My grandfather started it and they feel like it's this big family tradition or something. It's so much fucking work and if you're lucky, you break even. I don't want to do that with my life."

"You got that job with your uncle painting houses."

"That's just to get away. I didn't want to enlist and end up in Iraq like my cousins. But I don't want to paint houses for the rest of my life, either."

"You could start sending your drawings out. Maybe someone will publish Mad Cow."

He sighs. "Maybe."

"When you come to New York we can make the rounds at the publishing houses, you know, like Marvel Comics."

He gets up as he says, "That'd be really cool. You're a good kid, Molly. Thanks for the movie."

I just watch him from where I sit, willing him to stay. I say, "At least it got your mind off Julie, I hope. There's someone else out there for you."

He's heading to the door and I don't know how to stop him. Instead of good-bye, he just says, "I hope you're right. I mean it; I really hope you're right."

JUNE

It's one of our last chem labs, but Mark still hasn't shown up.

Mr. Sanchez says, "Molly, you can work on your own today or join another team."

I nod, knowing I won't join another team. It's then that Mark arrives, and Mr. Sanchez is not happy. "The bell rang five minutes ago," he says.

Mark shrugs and takes his place on the stool next to me. He takes my notebook out of his backpack and I open it anxiously, looking for a new work of art, some little drawing that shows that his feelings for me have changed, that he's finally beginning to realize the best thing that ever happened to him has been sitting right next to him his entire senior year. But there's no picture in it this time.

"'Sup?" I ask, greeting him in his own language. This is what my social studies teacher would call *culturally sensitive and appropriate*.

"'Sup," he mumbles. It's then I realize that things

are back to normal, like we hadn't shared *Spider-Man 3* at all.

We start in on our work, and finally he utters more than a grunt in my direction. He says, "I'm gonna need your help on the final. If that's okay."

Something like a wave of cold, clear water passes over me. "Sure, happy to help," I say. "Come on by after dinner."

When the final bell rings, I set the land-speed record for getting home. The house is a mess (of course); Mom's at Boss Burger, Dad's on the road, and Russ — who knows? *Please*, I think, *let Russ hang out with his loser friends somewhere else tonight!*

I look at the couch and the recliner; I run upstairs and grab some nice blankets to put over them so they match. I stack magazines into neat piles, I wash the dishes I can and hide the ones I don't have time to do. I need a shower, a new outfit, a new hairstyle, more makeup. I have to lose ten pounds before Mark shows up.

Panicked, I open the refrigerator. I can offer him diet pop, milk, or beer to drink, and leftovers to eat. I have to go to the store and get something good, like chips and dip or Doritos or real pop. But what if he shows up early and I'm not here?

Calm down, Molly. The shower — I have to shower first and work on my look. Then, time permitting, a trip to the store for something decent to offer him.

But no! Mom has the car!

I strategize: We'll study and then head out somewhere for a bite to eat. After we study, he should be hungry. We can *really* get to know each other. I need to prepare a list of subjects to discuss; I'm no good at improv. I need to rehearse.

No, first the shower.

I shampoo and condition, then scrub my face and armpits raw. I shave my legs and pits too fast and nick the skin, little pinpricks of blood everywhere. I dab and dab and dab at them. *This is wasting valuable time.*

I need the hair dryer to make my thin hair look thicker. But what if the doorbell rings and I don't hear it? I take a chance, blast the dryer on full, toss my head back and forth, praying for the correct height and volume and a nice, silky sheen.

What to wear, what to wear, what to wear? I toss my wet towel on my bed as I rifle though my drawers and closet. Nothing too nice — this is not *officially* a date — and nothing too casual that makes me look the way I always look whenever he sees me. Black is said to be slimming. A black top and jeans — I can't wear shorts — my legs are too cut up and, really, too white.

Earrings. I need a pair that doesn't make me look fat.

Perfume. I don't wear it. I run to Mom and Dad's room and scan her dresser for something subtle yet provocative. But all Mom has is Mary Kay! I need Calvin Klein! Where is Calvin Klein? There's some Insta-Tan. That could help even out my complexion.

I apply the Insta-Tan as calmly as I can, careful to even it out so it won't streak.

That's when I hear it: the doorbell.

Ohmigod, it's the doorbell.

No way is four-thirty P.M. *after dinner.*

Maybe he skipped dinner. That's a good sign, right? He couldn't wait to come over.

Oh God. He's here.

He's here, he's here, he's here!

What do I do?

I spray on some Mary Kay, but my aim is off and some gets in an eye and stings like hell.

He's here, he's here, he's here!

Another ring and I run down the stairs as I rub my eye, which is tearing. I stumble at the bottom step, slamming against the banister, but I don't fall.

A deep breath. I try to open the Mary Kay eye but all I can make it do is squint.

Another deep breath, and I open the door, a happy and alluring expression on my face.

"Hey, Molly-Pop."

And there he is.

Russ. My alleged brother.

Russell Jonathan Swain, fifteen-year-old ruiner of all things good and decent and pure.

I could just *kill* him.

He frowns, looks at me. "What's the deal with your eye? It's all red."

I grab him by a sleeve, yank him in the house, and slam the door. "Why did you ring the bell?"

"Chillax, I forgot my keys. Why do you smell like an old lady?"

I race back upstairs to rinse out my eye, shouting, "Just stay out of my way!"

He shouts back, "No problem!"

31

Mark never shows.

He blows off our study date, and when I wake up the next day, I'm horrified to discover my face is streaked in varying degrees of orange and my Mary Kay eye is still swollen and pink. In chem lab, Mr. Sanchez asks if I'm feeling well. I tell him I'm fine, just an allergic reaction to something. Donna Piambino laughs, asking if I got the license plate of the truck that hit me. I wouldn't mind her insults so much if she would just be a little more original with her put-downs. It's like I'm unworthy of any effort on her part.

But as Mom said when she pushed me out the door this morning, refusing to believe that I was sick, *This, too, shall pass.*

Mark arrives late, and he doesn't pick up on my annoyed vibe, doesn't even notice that my face looks like a melting Creamsicle or that I can only really see out of one eye. When he finally sits down on the stool next to mine and gets the hair out of his own eyes, he says, "'Sup?" Only then does he add, "Whoa, dude, what happened to you?"

Dude. He just called me *dude.* I'm mad, so I say, "I could ask you the same thing."

He nods, like he's listening to the radio. "Oh yeah, last night, sorry. Something came up."

A smarter person would not be thrilled by this apology. A smarter person would realize that if he was interested in me, he would have shown up last night, whether or not "something came up." I wonder what the something was — or, rather, *who* she was.

I say, "Back with Julie?"

He laughs. "You jealous?"

I'm glad my face is covered in orange or it would be red. "Of course not! I just assumed —" I try to say *just assumed* like I'm trying to being funny and nosy at the same time "— that you'd rather hang out with her rather than a chemistry book."

"Nothing like that. Just listening to some tunes and lost track of time." He pauses a moment before he adds, "So what happened to your face?"

"Allergic reaction," I mumble, hoping he'll drop it.

"Hope you feel better."

I redirect the conversation, such as it is. "How about you come over tomorrow night?" By then I should look like something approximating normal. For me.

He nods. "Cool."

I wonder what I see in this guy, but then he leans over and gives me a hug. He says, "You're awesome, Molly."

Since Mom's putting in so many hours at Boss Burger, I make dinner that night, trying to expand our horizons with spicy beef burritos that give Dad — who's only home for a couple of nights before his next trip — the runs.

I try to ignore the dishes for a few hours, hoping Russ will take the hint, but then I can't stand it any-more, so here I am up to my elbows in lemon-scented Dawn. The doorbell rings. I shout, "Russ, door."

Russ shouts, "Dad, door."

From upstairs comes Dad's voice like a cold front on the Fourth of July. "I'm on the crapper! Get off your lazy ass and get it yourself!"

Russ shouts, "Molly-Pop, door."

"You get it! And don't call me that!"

The doorbell rings again.

Russ shouts, "Can't stop now — Magneto's blowing everything to shit!"

I shake the water off my hands as best I can and storm into the sitting room. I glare at Russ, but he ignores me; he has computer-animated people to kill and maim.

I'd be better off talking to Magneto — at least *he's* interactive.

I open the door, already knowing it's going to be one of Russ's friends or maybe Dietz, Dad's friend, who always wants to drag Dad along for *a cold drink and a hot chick.* Dad never goes, so Dietz ends up inviting himself in to drink all of Dad's beer instead.

"'Sup?"

It's Mark.

"Hi."

We stare at each other.

I needed at least twenty-four hours to prepare for our study date. I say, "Mark, we agreed on *tomorrow* night." My hair's flat and my face is sweaty from the heat and a sink full of dishes.

He frowns, confused. "Did we? Dude, I'm sorry."

Tonight I was going to sit alone in my room with a quart of cold cream on my face in preparation for tomorrow night. I sigh. "Could you give me a minute?"

"Cool."

I leave him standing on the porch as I run upstairs.

Next, I pound on the bathroom door. Dad shouts, "Can't a man even get five minutes of peace in his own god-damned bathroom?"

I shout back, "You almost done?"

When Dad's really mad he doesn't say anything, so I have to make do with the mirror and brush in my bedroom.

I do the best I can, then fly back downstairs and out the front door. Russ hasn't even blinked.

It's a warm night. Mark is wearing a long-sleeved T-shirt and blue jeans, and I catch a whiff of marijuana off of them. I wonder why I didn't notice it right away.

He says, "Where you going?"

Oh, right. Inside. Studying. Books. "Come on in," I offer.

Now Dad's out of the bathroom, telling Russ to turn off his game, he wants to watch *Law & Order.* When we enter the sitting room, Dad looks at Mark suspiciously. He says, "Hello."

Mark replies with, "'Sup?"

Russ gawks as if I've just escorted his favorite band, Modest Mouse, into the room. He doesn't know what to make of me with a popular *dude.* Worlds are colliding.

I say to Dad, "We're just going up to my room to study."

Dad says, "Study in the kitchen." To Mark he says, "I didn't catch your name."

"Mark."

Dad frowns, trying to recall the name, and then he remembers. "Oh, so *you're* Mark. The lab partner."

Mark looks at me, and I smile, mortified.

Russ stands, all impressed, and says, "Hey, I'm Russ."

Mark says to Russ, "You go to Le Sueur High, don't you?"

"Sophomore." Russ sounds like he's the one with a crush on him.

"Cool."

In the kitchen Mark sits on the chair with duct tape and taps his fingers on the table. He hasn't brought his chemistry book with him, or a notebook, or even my notebook, which I lent him earlier. I say, "You want something to drink?"

"Brew, please."

I say, "Ah, my dad's not cool with me drinking. A pop?"

"Cool."

From the sitting room we hear, *"In the criminal justice system, the people are represented by two separate but equally important groups. . . ."* All we have is diet pop, so I crack open a can and put it in front of Mark.

He picks up the can and examines it before setting it back down. He says, "Molly, when you're in New York, do you think I can crash at your place once in a while? I mean, I'd like to visit the city, and the trains back from New York stop at midnight."

I sit across from him now. I try not to appear too eager as I say, "Of course. That'd be a lot of fun. Maybe we could go out for dinner and see a show."

He nods.

We look at each other for a moment and he smiles, which makes small dimples on his cheeks. He says, "You can tell me. Is that Insta-Tan, dude?"

I laugh. "Yes."

He shakes his head and says, "Don't worry, I won't tell anybody."

"Thanks. I guess we should get started. I'll get my chem book."

He motions for me to stay seated. "Ummm, I was thinking, I got so much catching up to do and you've been helping me out so much and stuff, and the final is the day after tomorrow and everything . . . "

I know where this is going. "You want me to write extra large on my final."

He nods his head gently. At long last I've verbalized our little arrangement.

I say, "Okay."

I expect him to say, *Cool, thanks*, and take off, but he surprises me by saying, "You wanna go for a walk or something?"

I say, "Yeah." Then I say, "Sure." Then I say, "Let's go!"

On the way out, Dad asks — from his recliner — "Where are you two headed?"

I say, "Just out for a walk."

He grunts. "Don't make it late."

Dad is usually a friendly guy, but I think he's been waiting for me to have a boyfriend so he can be over-protective and intimidating. Even though Mark's not my boyfriend (yet), I let Dad enjoy himself.

Russ says, really loudly, "Hey, Mark, see you at school, dude!"

Mark grunts.

We walk in silence, our destination a graveyard Mark says he likes to hang out in. From time to time I glance at him, trying to decide what makes him tick, but it's impossible. He has a blank, vacant look on his face. He never looks at me, just stares straight ahead, like he's waiting for something to appear on the horizon.

I've never been in Mound Cemetery at night. The tombstones are surrounded by trees, and we hear leaves rustle in the warm breeze. I recognize the names of some of the families in town inscribed on the headstones.

Mark sits right on a grave, leaning against its stone. He rests his elbows on his knees.

"This is kinda creepy," I tell him.

He smiles and says, "Don't worry, this is my grandfather's plot. He won't mind."

I sit down across from him. It seems to have gotten darker somehow, even though the sun set over an hour ago. He pulls a little flask from a pocket and asks, "Want some?" as he holds it between us.

"No, thanks."

He puts it to his lips, draining it.

We sit there in the dark. The silence makes me nervous, so I ask him, "When did your grandfather die?"

"A year ago April."

"I'm sorry." And then we're quiet again. I look around, taking in the marble stones and statues that leave long shadows of their own in the darkness. I say, "You hang out here a lot?"

"I'm sorry, we shoulda gone someplace else. You scared?"

"No."

"Sometimes I just don't wanna be around people." He runs a hand through his hair and I wish I had the nerve to do it for him. "And once in a while I talk to my granddad. You know, about how things are going."

"What do you tell him?"

"I tell him about school and stuff. Life. You know, the usual shit." Mark sighs and says, "I miss him. He was a good man. My dad works all the time and my mom's gone all Christian. There's no one I can really talk to, you know what I mean?"

I nod. "You can always talk to me."

He says, "You're sweet," and I have to remember to exhale. I lie down on my back and look up at the sky. A small gap opens in the cloud cover and I can see a few stars. Their light travels at 670 million miles per hour. It seems like a ray of light could have traveled that distance by the time Mark asks me, "You gonna miss Le Sueur?"

"I'm going to miss my family. Well, I mean, my mom and dad. Maybe I'll miss Russ. After a few months."

"Your dad doesn't like me."

"That's because he doesn't know you."

Mark looks up at the sky, too. He says, "I'm not gonna miss this place, not even one little bit."

"Is Montclair a lot nicer than Le Sueur?"

He looks back down at me. "Don't know, but I can't imagine it could be worse."

Mark passes the chem final, though we have a close call when Mr. Sanchez gets up from his desk and stands in front of our counter, his suspicious eyes moving from my face to Mark's, from my paper to Mark's. I try to ignore Mr. Sanchez and keep on working, but it's hard to focus on the problems at hand when a potentially much larger one is staring a hole in my head. After a few minutes Mr. Sanchez turns around and walks back to his desk, and Mark takes the opportunity to lean over and get a *really* good look at my paper. Occasionally, I glance at Donna Piambino to see if she's caught on, but she's preoccupied with her own final. She looks like she's on the verge of tears.

When the final grades come out, I'm named valedictorian.

Instead of speaking on the subject of quantum mechanics or string theory — which I know people would not understand — I focus my comments on global warming and the responsibility of our class to repair the damage done to the environment by our parents. I can't say it goes over incredibly well. One of the parents shouts "Tree hugger" when I'm done, causing Dad to get up and look around the gym's bleachers like he wants to punch whoever said it. The crowd applauds politely to move things along without incident.

Once all the names have been announced, Mom, Dad, and Russ congratulate me as the seniors, families, and friends congregate on the basketball court. Dad calls my speech thought-provoking, Russ thinks it was cool, and Mom wonders out loud why I couldn't have talked about enjoying life and looking on the bright side of things. She doesn't actually call me morose, but you can tell in her little expressions that she thinks I don't know how to enjoy myself.

Anyway, she's giving me one of her looks when I hear Mark shout, "Hey, Molly!"

Seeing him in a cap and gown instead of his usual dirty jeans and T-shirt makes me happy.

Russ says, "Hey, Mark, congrats, dude."

Mark says thanks, and I can tell he doesn't remember meeting Russ.

Then it happens: Mark sweeps me up in his arms and gives me a little spin. When he puts me down, he says, "Thanks so much for all your help." He hands me one of his sketches, saying, "This is for you."

It's a drawing of Mad Cow. His dialogue balloon says, *See you in the Big Apple!*

Mom and Dad don't see the caption, but still they look at each other.

We're joined now by a middle-aged man and woman, and I can tell they're Mark's parents. His mom has a sort of tragic look on her face, as if we were at a funeral instead of a graduation, and his father has the far-off expression I recognize from his son.

Once our parents introduce themselves (and Russ), Mark's mother says, "You're so lucky that your daughter will be around for at least three more months. Mark's leaving tomorrow."

Tomorrow?

I look at Mark, who is looking at his mother. He says, "Come on, it won't be that bad."

Tomorrow?

Dad says, "We're just lucky Molly will be close at the U."

Mark says, surprised, "She's going to Columbia. We're gonna be neighbors — right, Molly?"

I just say, "You're leaving tomorrow?"

Dad says, "You're going to New York?"

Russ says, "That is sooo cool, Molly-Pop!"

Mom says, "We'll talk about this later."

I whisper again to Mark, "You're leaving *tomorrow?*"

He says, "Got my ticket on the Greyhound."

His father says cryptically, "Yeah, who needs an extra set of hands on the farm during the summer?" Then he mumbles, "Corn's gonna turn our operation around, but where will *he* be?"

Mom gathers up Dad, Russ, and me for our celebration dinner. During the silent drive to the restaurant, I look at my picture of Mad Cow and wonder what a summer without seeing Mark has in store for me. Maybe time apart from him is just what I need. I don't know why I feel this way about him, but I can't help it. There's this part of me that holds on to the hope that if he got to know me, I mean *really* know me . . .

Dinner is stiff and pretty quiet, except for Russ, who thinks me going to New York is the coolest thing in the world. He talks about bands and clubs and "the scene." Dad just drinks beer after beer and Mom — well, Mom looks like Mom. When we get home, she goes straight to their bedroom, Russ takes off to a graduation party, and Dad sprawls out in his easy chair, a can of beer in his hand.

I take a seat on the couch and wait for him to say something.

Finally, he starts with, "So. Anything you want to say to me, Sweet Pea?" He's called me Sweet Pea for as long as I can remember. He worked for Green Giant, canning Le Sueur peas, when Mom got pregnant with me. They got married, moved into a trailer, then — *voilà* — six months later, his Sweet Pea arrives.

I turn to face him, and I can't help myself, I look at his gut, trying to decide how many pounds he's put on. I say, "Umm. I'm going to Columbia."

Dad says, "Get your old man another beer, Sweet Pea. This one is almost dead."

I head to the kitchen to get him another Pabst Blue Ribbon, along with a can of diet pop for me.

Dad takes a big swig of beer. After a minute, he says, "So you really want to go to New York?"

I say, "I've been talking about it for the last two years, Dad. You know I do. It's important to me."

He smiles. "I just thought, you know, maybe you'd reconsider."

I don't say anything.

He sighs, rubs his eyes with his free hand. "Sweet Pea, I'm so proud of you for getting that scholarship. You proved what I already knew: that you kick ass in the brains department. I can't even begin to tell you how proud I am." He pauses, takes a sip of his beer. "But now it's time to be practical. Come on, New York City? It's so far away. I think you'd be much happier at the U."

"Dad . . ."

"And it's dangerous. Folks are always getting themselves killed in New York. There's all those sex maniacs." This, I believe, is what you end up thinking when you watch too much *Law & Order*.

"Dad, please don't."

"At the U, I know you'd be safe. And you could come home whenever you want." I think being by himself so much when he's on the road makes Dad imagine all the things that can go wrong in life. When I was a kid he was freaked out about the millennium bug. He told us that at midnight on January 1, 2000, civilization would collapse. (We still have jugs of water and a box of PowerBars in the basement, just in case.) When nothing happened, he almost seemed disappointed, like his authority as a father had been usurped.

I hug myself. "I have my heart set on Columbia. I want to study something I love, and Columbia is the best place to do it."

He studies his beer can. "I just worry."

I say, "I know."

And that, I know, is where we're going to leave it.

JULY

The weeks go by slowly. I work for Green Giant at their research and development station, growing and harvesting peas and corn, which we put in cans and freeze with different saline solutions to see how the vegetables appear and taste after canning and freezing. It's not what you would call glamorous work, but it's a good match for me, helping things grow, nurturing them, discovering the best ways to preserve them. Other workers smoke on their breaks, talk about parties coming up or how the Twins are doing this season, but I prefer to spend my break time alone, watching the peas and corn in their rows, thinking about Mark and our imminent reunion.

I receive one postcard from him after he arrives in New Jersey.

> The ride out here took forever. Right now
> I mostly power-wash houses to prep them

for the paint. My uncle is a real slave driver,
so haven't had much time to look around.
Take care, mark

    I read it over and over, convinced that there's some secret code in his words, some hint or clue that I'm on his mind as much as he is on mine. But then no more postcards arrive.

AUGUST

The Minneapolis-St. Paul International Airport's Lindbergh Terminal is huge (Charles Lindbergh was from Minnesota, like F. Scott Fitzgerald, Prince, Al Franken, Bob Dylan, and Judy Garland). Eventually, we find the ticket counter for the discount airline that will fly me to LaGuardia, the airport in Queens, one of New York's five boroughs. Mom, Dad, and Russ come to see me off. After I make it through the metal detector, sniffle-y and red-eyed, I wave good-bye. I expected Mom to cry — which she does — but I'm surprised when Dad tears up. Russ just waves without enthusiasm. It's kind of sweet, actually. I wag my finger at Russ; I never thought my little brother would be sad to see me go.

At the gate I sit by myself and read Mark's postcard over and over again. I picture him dripping wet from the power wash, his skin dark brown from spending so much time outdoors.

I pray all through the liftoff, only stopping when the plane levels off at thirty thousand feet. I've only flown twice in my entire life, when my Grammy Hautman died. We all went to Pennsylvania for the funeral (except Dad — he had literally just pulled out of the driveway for Kansas City). Aunt Aggie and Aunt Betty came, too, and got drunk on the plane on about twenty of those little bottles of booze. At the wake they said they had the most expensive hangovers of their lives.

I know I shouldn't be afraid to fly. I understand the mechanics of flight (a good analogy is to think of the sky as an ocean and the plane as a ship), and I know the statistics (flying is much safer than driving a car). But I can't help it.

For my going-away, Russ got me a Modest Mouse T-shirt. I'm wearing it right now, as I sit in the center seat, not that the businessmen on either side of me (who are kind of jerks because they took the armrests for themselves) have a clue that Modest Mouse is a band, popular but not overly commercial, which makes them all the cooler. That is my goal for my new life in New York: to be popular, but not overly commercial.

I wish Mark were here. I imagine him in the seat next to me, holding my hand as he looks out the window. We talk about our new life together in New York, how we'll decorate our tiny apartment, whether we should get one cat or two, what we'll name them.

I'm trying to take my mind off of Mark by reading a bit of my book when one of the businessmen, bored with his laptop, looks at my copy of *The Fabric of the Cosmos* and says, "You understand that stuff?"

I smile, even though he's still hogging the armrest. "Not all of it, but a lot of it."

"I tried to read it. Put me right to sleep."

How can a book on space, time, and the texture of reality bore *anyone?* "I find it really fascinating."

He smirks at me. "You going to be an astronaut, then?"

I think I roll my eyes, but I hope not. "A quantum physicist."

"I see. You're in college, then?"

"Columbia."

He nods, impressed. "When I was your age I was studying poetry."

This gets my attention. "They have a physics-for-poets class at Columbia."

"Do they have a poetry class for physicists?"

"I don't know."

He smiles, says, "They should," and returns to his laptop.

We hit a bump. Nothing big, just enough to shake the plane a little.

I open my purse and pull out the picture of Mark that I cut out of my yearbook. His photo is in a little acrylic frame I got so it won't get damaged or smudged. Mark's actually smiling in the photo. If you look at it closely you can see there's a tiny little gap between his front teeth, hardly noticeable, and for some reason I think it makes him look all the more handsome.

The businessman with the laptop notices and asks, "That your fella?"

I blush, and after a moment I say, "Yes."

"How long you two been together?"

I think about this before I say, "Four years."

He frowns. "You don't look old enough."

"High school sweethearts," I tell him.

He says, "Oh, I see. . . ."

I give him a knowing look as I say, "He proposed when we graduated, but I thought we should wait a while before we got engaged."

The businessman nods seriously. "That's probably a good idea. I married young, and it didn't last. Neither did the next two. But I think I got it right this time."

I stare at him too long before I say, "Oh."

After what feels like days, we finally approach New York. People look out the windows at the Manhattan skyline, which seems to go on forever, like a forest of skyscrapers. I've never seen anything like it. When we make our descent into LaGuardia, my heart's beating too fast. Once the plane comes to a stop on the runway, the flight attendant gets on the PA and says, "Welcome to New York, where the local time is four-forty P.M."

A crowd has formed around the baggage carousel. In addition to my purse and my backpack (both of which I managed to squeeze on board), I have two giant suitcases (Aunt Aggie gave me her old Samsonites, which are hard-sided and weigh a ton). The suitcases are full of clothes, most of them new. Mom took me out to Wal-Mart for my college wardrobe, and I do have to say that what we picked out is pretty stylish for a Le Sueur gal on a tight budget.

Now that I see my suitcases emerge from the chute I wonder what I was thinking. Dad and Russ had to carry them for me in Minneapolis, and even Dad complained about how heavy they were. I grunt as I lift one, and then the other, off the carousel, nearly swinging the second bag into a baby carriage.

"Hey, watch what you're doing! You coulda hit my kid!"

I blush and look apologetically at the baby's mother, who's scowling at me as she holds a cell phone to her ear. She says to whoever's on the other end, "Some stupid bitch almost hit Ethan with her fucking suitcase!"

I wince as I slink away (it was an *accident*, she didn't have to swear), barely able to get any forward momentum going, thanks to the backpack that I stuffed too full, the old Samsonites, and my purse. I make it about twenty feet in the direction of the bus (they have these helpful signs with pictures of buses on them, probably for people who don't speak English, which is a *lot* of people at this airport) before I have to set down the bags and rest. Everyone races around me with little bags on wheels that they pull by a handle as they talk on cell phones.

I grab the bags. I lift. I walk. I stop.

It takes me forever to get to the bus stop. It feels like eight million degrees outside and the air smells bad. My only bit of luck is that a blue-and-white M60 bus pulls right up so I don't have to wait for one in the fumes. When the doors open, a crowd of people — white, black, brown, and Asian — swarm inside. Once I'm at the doors, the bus driver looks at me skeptically.

"You're gonna drag all that shit on my bus, honey?" he asks. He's an older black man with a gray beard and a newspaper in his lap. We have lots of Mexican people in Le Sueur but only one black family, and their kids aren't my age.

I blush. "Yes, sir."

He sighs. "Get on, then, if you think you can manage it."

The entrance is too narrow for both Samsonites, so I have to drag them on one at a time. People are shooting me really nasty looks and I'm sweating, even though the bus is air-conditioned. The driver pulls forward before I can even pull some change out of my pocket, so I grab a pole as I fall backward, hitting someone behind me with the backpack.

"Yo!"

"Sorry," I mutter. There are no seats near the front, so I have to portage my suitcases to the back as the bus moves. Well, sort of moves. Mostly it's start, stop, honk, start, stop, honk. The driver seems to be reading the paper and driving at the same time, which makes me nervous. Finally, a Hispanic man with tattoos everywhere helps me drag the second Samsonite to the back of the bus. I tell him "*Muchos gracias*," and he just laughs a little, and tells me, "No prob." We stop at other terminals and more people get on, some of them looking at me because my backpack takes up the seat next to me and the Samsonites block the aisle. I want to look out the windows but I just stare at my feet.

I realize I forgot to ask the driver to let me know when we get to Columbia. Say what you want about Le Sueur, it's a hard place to get lost. We stop and more people get on. The air's thick. Passengers talk on cell phones in English and Spanish and other languages I don't recognize. I should have taken a cab, but they're so expensive and Dad told me that cabbies take their passengers miles out of the way so they can charge them more.

I should be excited that I'm finally in New York, but all we do is sit in traffic and it's hard to do anything but worry. We stop every block and nobody seems to be getting off, but more people get on. I balance my backpack on my lap and a heavy brown woman takes the seat next to me. People are standing in the aisles and a really fat white man straddles one of my Samsonites as best he can. I start to *really* sweat now, and all I hear are passengers on their cells, car horns, and the driver yelling at the pedestrians who run in front of the bus.

I look at my watch. It's been nearly thirty minutes and we've maybe made it a couple of miles. Even if I wanted to look out the windows I can't; people are packed in too tightly.

I won't know where to get out.

What if I miss my stop and they make me get out in a really bad neighborhood?

Why did I pack so much stuff?

I don't know where I am. I mean, I know from the Web where I am on the map: heading down Astoria Boulevard in Queens on my way to Harlem (the bus takes 125th Street from the East Side to the West Side until it turns left on Amsterdam Avenue and enters Morningside Heights). So I could locate myself, say, from some vantage point high above the city. But here, on the ground, I'm nowhere to be seen.

The bus stops again, and somehow more people press themselves in. I smell B.O.

I miss Mark. I wish I were power-washing houses with him. At least I'd be cool.

I miss Mom. And Dad. And even Russ. I'm pitting out the Modest Mouse shirt. A raggedy black man dressed way too warmly for the weather hops aboard, carrying a stuffed plastic shopping bag. He's shouting now, "I need change for thirty-six nickels! Who got change for thirty-six nickels?"

I do the math. Since a nickel can only be divided

into cents, the equation is thirty-six times five, which equals a hundred eighty pennies. Then I think: That makes no sense. If you had thirty-six nickels you would probably want one dollar and three quarters, while keeping one nickel.

I shouldn't have come here.

The bus stops and somehow even more people get on.

I sit, I wait. I panic. Finally, the bus makes a left-hand turn. My stop should be coming up soon.

If not for the fact that the bus driver announces that we've arrived at West 116th Street, I probably would have spent the night on the M60. But, thankfully, I've made it to the corner of 116th and Broadway. Regrettably, I can't tell which direction the John Jay Residence Hall is, so I just drag my Samsonites and walk with deliberate steps, pretending to know where I'm headed. The streets feel like the inside of a Crock-Pot on simmer, and the air smells like exhaust. There's traffic, concrete, and people who know where they are, where they're going. I pretend I'm one of them, but all I want to do is cry.

That's when I hear a voice, calling after me.

"Hi — you here for the move-in?"

This is probably what muggers say to identify out-of-towners. I keep walking. Or trying to walk.

"Hello? Are you here for the move-in?"

I'm covered in my own sweat, I can barely carry my suitcases, my backpack, and this thing I call a purse. But worst of all, I don't know which way to turn. I say, "Yeah. I'm moving into the John Jay Residence today."

"You're going the wrong way." The guy wears a T-shirt and cargo shorts along with a name tag that identifies him as a member of the college's orientation staff. He looks like he may be Pakistani or Indian, and his thick dark hair is pulled back from his face in a pony-tail. "Don't worry — I'm supposed to be on the lookout for lost first-years."

"Oh. Thanks."

He points to the Samsonites. "Can I carry one of those for you?"

As soon as I hand it to him he regrets the offer.

When I first walk into the John Jay Residence, I'm awed by the high ceilings, the chandeliers, the fireplace, the grand piano. It's a very deceptive way to introduce someone to the building. To get to know the real John Jay, I have to go upstairs to the dorm rooms. I quickly discover that I have a small and dingy single room in a fifteen-story building reserved for first-years. Most everyone has a single, and all the doors are open as students and parents unload and unpack. There's a lot of laughter and some tears as mothers and fathers say good-bye to sons and daughters. But mostly there's energy, an excitement that runs from room to room like an electrical current.

And then there's me, sitting in my room. Thankfully, the phone works so I've called Mom and Dad to let them know I've arrived safely, but I have no idea what to do next. I take out the picture of Mark and put it on my desk, where I can see it from my bed. Next, I open a Samsonite and take out the laptop that Mom and Dad and allegedly Russ gave me for my birthday in July. I wanted to take it as a carry-on, but Dad told me how laptops get stolen all the time at airports when you go through the security check, something he had heard on a news magazine show, the ones that always start off with *Are YOU At Risk?* or *Are YOUR Children Safe?*

I look around my room, trying to decide the best place to keep the laptop so it doesn't get stolen. Then I check the locks on my door. I peek my head out into the hallway, and already the other residents' doors look like photo albums, full of pictures of groups of girls with their arms around one another, smiling and laughing at the camera.

"Modest Mouse, I love them!"

I look down at my T-shirt and realize whoever just spoke must be addressing me. I say, "Me, too." Truth be told, I prefer the Dixie Chicks.

"Looks like we're neighbors! I'm Lily." She's Asian and I'm embarrassed to admit I was expecting an accent.

"Molly," I tell her. "Molly Swain. From Le Sueur, Minnesota."

She claps her hands together. "Oh my God, I love that film *Fargo*. It's a classic. Oh, my last name's Monteleone." She shakes my hand as she says, "I'm from Grosse Pointe. Have you ever seen *Grosse Pointe Blank*?"

"You have to drive to Mankato or the Cities if you want your pick of movies."

She laughs. *"Man-kay-toe.* I love the way you talk just like Margie."

"Who's —"

"I think I've seen every film ever made. I've seen *Fargo* seven times! It's in my top fifty films of the twentieth century, right behind *On the Waterfront*, just ahead of *Hiroshima Mon Amour.* What will you be studying?"

"Physics."

"Film studies for me — big surprise, right? Do you have a favorite film?"

I don't go to movies much. "I liked *Titanic.*"

Her smiles freezes like Leonardo DiCaprio in the North Atlantic. "Oh."

An older white couple appears next to her. The woman says, "Honey, let's get something to eat, I'm famished."

The man says, "Who's your friend?"

Lily says, "Mom, Dad, this is Molly from Man-kay-toe, Minn-ah-sew-tah."

"Actually, it's Le Sueur."

The woman frowns. "Le Sueur peas?"

"Yes."

The couple laughs. Lily's mother says, "You're from the Valley of the Jolly Green Giant!" Then, Lily's father sings, "Ho-ho-ho, Green Giant," and they laugh some more.

I turn red and stare at my feet.

Next they ask me if I'd like to join them for a late dinner, their treat.

I have to leave my room if I want to eat, so I say yes.

It's late, I'm exhausted from the flight, the bus ride, moving in, making small talk with Lily's parents, basically everything that's happened in one very long day. This morning I was in my own bed in my own home. Now I'm in a small room on West 114th Street in Manhattan where I live on a floor with over forty first-years, all of whom are talking and laughing in the hallway.

I can't help myself; I managed to get Mark's phone number off his mother before I left, so I call him to let him know I've arrived. Also, I'm desperate to talk to someone from back home and I can't let my mom and dad know I'm already homesick.

"Hello?"

He actually picks up.

"Mark, it's Molly."

"Hey, Molly! 'Sup? You in New York?"

Just the sound of him makes me happy. "Got here today. This city is like . . . I can't describe it. It's overwhelming." Then I add, "It's been a while since I've heard from you. You didn't even send your address."

He mumbles, "Summer's our busy season — all exterior work. I haven't had much time for other things."

"You paint after the sun sets?"

"Uh, you know . . . gotta do inventory. And invoices and shit. And clean the brushes and shit."

Just like on the farm, they're working him stupid. I decide to change the topic. I take a deep breath and say, "Do you want to come into the city? Classes don't start till next week. I don't know, we could go to Central Park or Times Square or the top of the Empire State Building, you know, where Mad Cow fought the biplanes."

"Huh?"

"You know, that drawing you did."

"Oh, yeah."

Another deep breath. "So, do you want to see the sights?"

"Dude, this weekend is really bad — we're way behind schedule and I haven't had a day off in weeks. My uncle took on way too many jobs."

"Oh . . ."

"But give me your number. I'll call you."

So I do, and then we say our good-byes. I get ready for bed, passing girls in the hall on my way back and forth to the bathroom. They laugh and talk and some say hello, but I just nod, anxious to get some sleep.

The thing about Le Sueur is, it's quiet. With the exception of when the bars close on the weekends, you can fall asleep in perfect silence.

Manhattan is not quiet. Especially not John Jay, or JJ, as it's popularly known.

So I lie in my bed in the dark as the shrieks of laughter echo in the hall.

And I cry very quietly, so no one can hear.

The next morning Lily knocks on my door, accompanied by a girl named Jessie who lives on our hall, and together they invite me out for coffee. Lily announces that Café 212 will be our new hangout. As soon as we get there, Lily and Jessie are talking at the same time and drinking coffee by the gallon.

Lily says to Jessie, "Molly's studying physics."

Jessie makes impressed *oooh* sounds before she asks me, "Why physics?"

I say, "Well, when I was little I loved astronomy, and then it was biology. I guess I've been hooked on quantum physics since I first saw *The Elegant Universe*."

Jessie, who comes from San Francisco, practically

screams, "Oh my God! I absolutely loved that series! String theory is sooo cool! And that guy teaches here!"

That's all I need. I'm in. We start talking for hours about everything, absolutely everything: our families, where we come from, our impressions of New York and Columbia, and boyfriends. (I'm relieved that I'm not the only one without a boy back home.) We talk about the high school cliques and Lily announces that I was an indie kid because I was wearing a Modest Mouse T-shirt when we met.

"So, what other bands do you like?" Jessie asks me.

There are choices everyone has to make in life, including how to present your past to the people in your present. Time is the one dimension we cannot travel back and forth in, as much as we wish we could. Lily and Jessie are friendly, welcoming, trusting. I could make up anything about what I was like in high school to make myself more impressive than I really am. But, as my dad says, *Once you lie, you have to remember to stick with it. That's the tricky part.*

I say, "Actually, my brother got the shirt for me. I wasn't indie . . . just left out. You know, the uncool, lonely, smart kid. I even had my own personal bully right up until graduation."

They both look at me sympathetically, and Lily reaches for my hand, takes it in her own. She says, "Well, sistuh-woman-sistuh, your new friends kick bully ass. Let me at 'em!"

The first week is a revelation. We stay up too late, we talk and talk and talk, we complete our orientation, we sightsee via the subway and buses. This city and its people are like nothing else. Yes, time is a dimension that we can't move around in as we can in the other three dimensions (the dimensions we can perceive, anyway), but our perception of it can change, we can experience it in different ways, we say it drags or flies by, and now I realize that the problem with time when you are essentially friendless is that is appears static, unchanging. But here, in this city, with Lily and Jessie, it's morphed into a cheetah. The things I say don't sound stupid to me anymore, now that people actually hear my words and respond to them.

I guess this is what it feels like to be included. I wish it for everyone.

Except Donna Piambino.

SEPTEMBER

It's the weekend before classes start, so Jessie has decided that we have to have a girls' night out on the town. Jessie has seen every episode of *Sex and the City* (I have to admit, I haven't seen a single one) and thinks she's most similar to Carrie, who she tells me is the creative one who also has had some bad luck in the love department. Jessie has long, flowing, light-brown hair that's streaked here and there with pink; I think Russ would like her.

When Jessie stops by my room, she takes one look at me and decides I need some help. "You need to adjust your look. It's a bit too . . . *earnest* for a club. I have a smoky brown eye shadow that would look amazing with your eyes and hair and would make you look a little more defined. Your skin is fair and I think that works for you. Are you Irish?"

"Dutch, German, Scottish, Polish, Welsh. And if you go back far enough, there's a drop or two of Chippewa."

Jessie says, "Hmmm. Your hair . . ."

I always just wear it parted down the middle or in a ponytail, since it's so flat.

She says, "Let's find you a stylist who can volumize" (is that a word?) "and shape your hair so your face has more angles."

Lily appears in the doorway, looking like a super-model outfitted in a black miniskirt, black earrings, and black spike heels. I, on the other hand, am wearing a summer floral print dress from Wal-Mart that I was proud of until exactly five seconds ago. Lily looks at her nails (painted black, of course) and asks, "You guys ready?"

Jessie, who is dressed entirely in gray, tells her it's much too early to go to the clubs (it's nine on a Saturday night) and besides, she has to do a quick makeover on me. She piles my hair on top of my head and lets it drop. She stares at me like I'm a blank canvas just waiting for her to fill me in. She says, "I know you guys want to go to Midtown, but there's this *amazing* club I heard about in Soho that we *have* to go to. And I *know* we can get in — the bouncer is a good friend of a good friend of a good friend of mine back in San Fran."

Lily says, "Cool. We're in your hands — aren't we, Molly?" I nod as Lily inspects my room, shaking her head. "You have an entire wall of corkboard and not a single poster or picture up." Her eyes shift to my desk. "Nice! Is that that Mark guy you told us about?"

"Yeah, that's him."

Lily hands the picture to Jessie. "Feast your eyes upon this magnificent specimen."

Jessie takes one look and starts fanning the space between her legs with her free hand.

Lily says, "So you guys have never made out?"

I say, "No. He doesn't even know I like him. Well, maybe he knows. It's complicated."

Jessie says, "Complicated never looked so good," as she takes my hand and leads Lily and me down the hall to her room. Lily watches as Jessie organizes her makeup on the desk. Jessie mumbles, "Lessee, foundation, shadow, mascara, gloss." She looks at me for a long moment like a contractor surveying a job, and I imagine she's wondering if I am a complete tear-down and rebuild.

Lily must sense my tension because she says, "Maybe just some lip gloss?"

Jessie shakes her head seriously. "Now, that won't do," she judges. Then she turns to me and says, "Oh. Sorry. I just meant . . ." and then she trails off. Leaning over me, she says, "Close your eyes and relax." To Lily, she says, "Foundation," like she's saying "Scalpel" in an operating room.

The procedure takes longer than I could have imagined. I hear Jessie ask Lily to hand her things, and occasionally she corrects Lily, saying, "Autumn Ash number fourteen, not eight."

When they lead me to the mirror, I think of Cinderella after her transformation by her fairy godmother. Then I see my reflection. I'm slightly alarmed, and a little disappointed.

Jessie says excitedly, "What do you think? Really highlights your eyes and helps define the cheekbones."

By *defines the cheekbones* she really means *creates the illusion of cheekbones*. This is a makeover they should use in the Witness Protection Program.

Still, I think I look a little better.

Now if only I don't sweat it all off. . . .

The cab ride takes forever, but I don't mind. As Lily and Jessie discuss guys, I sit quietly, staring out the window, taking in the people on the streets, the buildings, the bright lights of the traffic, the disappointed looks of pedestrians trying to hail cabs as ours slowly drives by. There's a soundtrack to this city — the cars, their horns, the occasional sirens — and it's charming, in its own way.

Finally, we arrive in Soho. The trip costs a fortune, but Lily treats. She hasn't said so, but she's figured out that money is a major issue for me. Still, I feel bad that she feels like she has to pay. But not bad enough to open my purse, which, compared to Jessie's and Lily's, looks more like a laundry bag with synthetic leather straps.

The club is called Push Room, and at first I'm afraid Jessie's bouncer won't be working tonight and we'll be carded and not allowed inside. But when I see the crowd outside smoking cigarettes, I'm afraid Jessie's bouncer *is* working tonight and that we *will* be allowed inside. The crowd looks older, but then so do we with all this stuff on our faces. There are no other summer floral print dresses anywhere. The men are what Jessie calls "metrosexuals," and the women, with just one exception (yours truly), look like models. Jessie says, "What'd I tell you — hot guys with money, honeys."

Of course Jessie's bouncer is working. Unlike the other people who have their ID cards swiped, we're just waved in once Jessie tells him who she is. And after she slips him some money.

We enter, and there's a loud *thumpa-thumpa* techno beat and soft neon lighting that runs through thin tubes along the walls. We have to speak loudly to be heard. I say, "The bartenders here are really handsome."

Jessie's dismissive. "*Pffft.* They're all actors or models or actor-slash-models."

"Wow," I say, "why are they bartending?"

Jessie and Lily laugh, but it's not the vicious kind my radar is designed to detect. Jessie says, "To make a living. Molly, honey, this is New York. The bartenders, the waiters, the waitresses — they're all here for something else: acting, singing, modeling, dancing, painting, writing, sculpting. You know, all the things people want to do but can't make a living at."

I look at the bartenders. The one with long hair and thin lips looks a little like Mark. I point at him and ask, "What do you think he does?"

Lily and Jessie are horrified. Lily says, "Molly! Never point at someone in a club. Play it cool, sistuh-woman-sistuh."

Still, they look at him.

"Actor," Jessie says.

But Lily's not so sure. "I don't know, I'm getting a poet vibe. He moves like a metaphor."

I don't know what she means. I'd ask, but I've

already pointed in a club; I don't want to look like a complete idiot. I'm feeling generous with my new friends and still bad that Lily paid for the cab, so I say, "What do you want to drink? I'm buying."

Obviously, Lily and Jessie have already discussed my finances between themselves. Jessie says, "Tonight's on us, honey."

But I insist, and they agree I can buy the first round. We find a tall table and pull up three bar stools. When a waiter (even better-looking than the bartenders) brings us three enormous apple martinis (Jessie's suggestion), I pull out my wallet and ask "How much do I owe you?"

"Forty-two."

"Dollars?"

"No, sweetheart, magic beans."

At about the speed of light, Lily hands him her credit card and says, "Just run a tab, please."

Jessie and Lily raise their glasses for a toast, but I just sit there, stunned. I say, "These are fourteen dollars *each.*"

Lily says, "Come on, live a little."

I lift my glass, which could be a comfy home for a goldfish, and we clink our glasses together. Jessie says, "To the three *E*s: Lil-ee, Moll-ee, and Jess-ee!"

I say, "Oh, that's really cute," and then we take a sip of our apple martinis. I swallow and gasp.

Lily says, "They do have martinis in Le Sueur, don't they?"

I catch my breath. "My father just drinks PBR."

They look at each other, confused.

Lily says, "There's not one single Asian guy in this place."

I say, "Oh, aren't you allowed to date outside your race?"

Jessie nearly spits out her drink.

Lily laughs, says, "Yeah, my white parents insist I only date nice Chinese boys. Honestly, Molly. I just think Asian guys are hot. Besides, white boys always want me to be shy and giggle softly in public and then they expect me to be a bitch-in-heat in bed."

I blush. *"Lily!"*

She shrugs. "It's the truth."

By the second round, I'm really enjoying myself. We talk about boys, and Jessie and Lily wonder how long it will take before I lose my virginity. I say, "Oh, I don't need to do that anytime soon." I take another sip, and then say, "When Mark and I would just talk, like that night in the graveyard, that was enough for me. It was so nice. I really liked it when we would just talk, you know."

Lily says, "We know."

I fan myself; it feels stuffy in here. I lean toward Lily and say, "Isn't it nice? When you just talk? I think that's very nice."

Lily nods.

I say, "Like that night in the graveyard with Mark."

The crowd has gotten thicker and it's *really* hot in here. I have to fan my armpits every once in a while.

Jessie orders a third round, peach martinis this time. I say, "Do you know that, in the quantum cafe, if you order a drink, the bartender says, 'I'll try.'" I look at Lily; she is such a lovely person, really, the best, and I ask her, "You know why?" And then I look at Jessie; she is such a lovely person, really, the best, and I ask her, "You know why?"

Lily glances at Jessie, who, for some reason, looks like she wants to laugh. Jessie says, "Because in the quantum cafe, everything is based on probability, not immutable law."

"Oh my God," I tell her, "that's it! That's exactly it!"

Lily frowns. "What are you two talking about?"

Jessie says, "It was in that series *The Elegant Universe*. What's-his-face —"

"Brian Greene!" I say. "The man's a genius."

Jessie looks at me, and then back at Lily. "Yeah, Brian Greene uses it to demonstrate the theory."

"It's soo cool," I tell them.

As we finish our third round, we're all laughing hysterically. We say, "The three *Es* rock!" and "Three *Es* can't be wrong!" Guys ask Lily to dance, but she tells them to come back once they've grown eyelids. She's so funny! Jessie dances once in a while, but she doesn't mean it, you can tell, I mean, you can tell. She just wants to dance. That's all. She enjoys dancing. You can tell. Nothing wrong with that. No, sir.

On the cab ride home we giggle and Lily tells me, "You're shlurring your speech. Don't you evuh drink?"

I say, "Oh my God, am I? I can't tell. Have I been slurring all week?"

They burst out laughing.

Jessie says, "Oh my God, I just drooled on myself."

We all laugh.

When we get to JJ, good old JJ in good old Morningside Heights, we tumble into the elevator and Lily has to sit on the floor, she's laughing so hard.

In our hall, we try to be quiet, we say "*Shhh*" to one another and that makes us laugh all the harder. We group-hug our good night.

And then I'm on my bed and looking at my picture of Mark, sweet, wonderful, beautiful Mark, who I love more than anyone else. I dial his number but I get it wrong and whoever answers is really crabby. I get it right on the second try.

"Hello?"

"*Mark!* It's Molly!"

"Molly? Do you know what time it is? You're lucky I'm up. If you'd woken up my aunt and uncle —"

"How are you, honey? You little honey-bunny! Do you miss me? 'Cause I sure miss you! Yes I do!"

"Molly, are you drunk?"

I laugh. "We had martinis with apples and peaches in them."

"How many?"

I think really hard. "I dunno. How many is four?"

Mark's laughing and I'm laughing and the room's spinning.

In string theory, the belief is that the smallest component parts of everything — you, me, my desk, Manhattan — are unimaginably tiny strings or loops of vibrating energy. Brian Greene calls it the *cosmic symphony*, comparing the vibrations of these tiny bits of energy to the strings of a violin when a bow is run across them.

This morning, the bow that plays my strings could make you want to rip out your eardrums.

I have never been so miserable in my life, and I include my time in ninth grade with Donna Piambino.

Why, God, why?

Never again.

I swear off booze.

Someone, please, just put the pillow over my face and smother me. I'd do it myself, but I can't move without throwing up.

I look at the clock, and the dimension that is time, the one we cannot move forward or backward in, has decided to stop entirely. I will it to be four P.M., when, from my experience observing Dad's hangovers, I will feel better.

I lean over, I throw up in the trash can again. Something's jabbing into my arm and I discover that it's my picture of Mark in the acrylic frame, which somehow ended up on my bed.

Oh, Mark. Thank God you can't see me right now. I'm not even sure I believe in God, but just in case he or she exists, I thank him or her that Mark can't see me, Mom can't see me, and, best of all, Dad can't see his Sweet Pea with a line of saliva hanging from her mouth over a trash can that smells like week-old roadkill baking in the sun.

Lily appears in the doorway. Evidently, I never turned the dead bolt.

She says, "Jesus, it smells like somebody died in here."

I moan, "Someone did."

She smiles, but just a little bit. "The secret is to drink a lot of water and take a couple of aspirin before you go to bed. . . . Oh, who am I kidding? I feel like shit." Lily sits on the edge of the bed and puts her head in her hands. "I wonder how Jessie's doing."

"We should go check."

But neither of us moves.

After a while, Lily wipes her face and says, "I'm going back to bed. We *have* to feel better, we just *have* to. I can't begin my first day of classes hungover." She stands and slowly staggers out of the room, muttering, "Why? Why?"

There are things I wanted to do today and I can't do any of them. I just curl up in the fetal position and try to sleep. I don't even call Mark to find out what I said to him last night.

Thankfully, the Three *Es* are feeling fine by the first day of class. I sit in the back rows of classrooms while professors review their syllabi and warn us about cell phones in class and attendance and plagiarism and academic integrity. Today was Masterpieces of Western Literature and Philosophy (better known as Lit Hum) and University Writing (known everywhere else as freshman composition). Not exactly quantum mechanics, and I don't have any classes with Brian Greene, but we're all expected to complete what is called the "core curriculum" our first two years, which includes phys ed (I had hoped those awful days were behind me) and, of all things, a swimming test. Dad said it's because Manhattan's an island, and I told him that that was ridiculous, and then he got a little annoyed and told me that of course he was just teasing me. Anyway, for phys ed I decided on a strength training course in the hopes that added muscle will help me burn off fat. I just want to lose ten pounds. But it's hard; I already gained weight orientation week, and everyone's talking about the Freshman Fifteen, the number of pounds you gain from dorm food.

Still, I'm happy with the courses I'm taking,

although the workload is so different from high school that I'm a little terrified. Okay, a LOT terrified. And as someone planning to be a physicist, I resent having to read *The Iliad.* Happily, Frontiers of Science is part of the core curriculum, too, so all the humanities people's turn to suffer is coming up.

The Three *Es* meet Tuesday morning at Café 212 for coffee to discuss the day ahead, and Tuesday evening we eat dinner together to compare notes on how the day went. Our discussion lasts late into the evening, save the breaks we take to try and find answers to our questions on the Internet.

When I finally work up the nerve to try to reach Mark on Thursday evening, he's not home and I get his aunt instead. She needs to work on her phone manners.

Time speeds by, and days turn into weeks. Mark is *never* home — I swear, it's like he's a missing person. They should put his picture on milk cartons. On my bad days I imagine that I said something *really* stupid to him when I was drunk, maybe even told him I loved him. But mostly I think I just imagined calling him that night. I'm walking back to JJ from Hamilton Hall with a quick stride, smoky brown eye shadow on my eyelids and smoky brown gloss on lips, my shorter, textured hair bouncing in time with my steps. I decide that maybe this time apart from Mark is a good thing — when we do see each other, I'll be thinner and more attractive. When I arrive at my floor, I open the door covered with photos of Lily and Jessie and me. Lily has left a message: She is over her crush on the Vietnamese-American guy in her writing class, whose favorite film, she discovered to her horror, is *The Fast and the Furious.*

I sit at my desk, reading and Googling for my classes. Every day or so, I Google Mark, but nothing shows up on the screen. So I go back to taking notes. I make citations in the MLA format; I check my progress against the various syllabi. Finally, I lie on my bed and open Dante's *Divine Comedy*, which I know will make me fall asleep. That's when someone knocks on my door, which, in spite of my dad's warnings, I've left unlocked.

"Yeah," I shout.

Jessie, in her T-shirt and jogging shorts, opens the door with an odd expression on her face. She asks in a peculiar tone of voice, like she knows something that I don't, "How are *you* this evening, Miss Molly?"

I smile at her, confused. "Fine."

She looks at me with a wily grin. She says in a sing-songy voice, "I have a little surprise for you."

I rub my eyes, struggling to stay awake. "What is it?"

"Guess. Come on, it'll be fun."

I groan. "Jessie, it's nearly two in the morning. And I still have to read Dante."

"Just one little guess. Just one little, itsy-bitsy guess. Just one little, isty-bitsy, teensy-weensy guess. Just one little —"

I close *The Divine Comedy*. "How much coffee have you had?"

"Way too much. I was on my way down for more when I stopped in the lobby. Here's a clue: It's very pretty and very quiet."

"A museum?"

Jessie laughs. "Let me try again." She clears her throat, squints her eyes, and says in a deep, soft voice, "'Sup, dude?"

"I don't under —"

"Oh, I can't stand it anymore! Here!"

And then she pushes Mark Dahl into my doorway.

I see his handsome face, a deep tan from the summer, his drowsy eyes, his thin lips, which are pouting. He wears his uniform, a pair of jeans, sneakers, and a long-sleeve T-shirt.

He says so softly that I almost miss it, "Hey, Molly."

Jessie says, "I found him in the lobby. He was about to call your room when I recognized him, so I went ahead and signed him in! He's just as cute as his picture!"

I could cry. I get up and hold out my arms, and we embrace. The feel of his arms holding me tight is like nothing else.

He says again, even quieter than before, "Hey, Molly."

I say, savoring the feel of his body against mine, "Hey, Mark."

I squeeze him hard and nestle my head under his strong jaw. Here is where time can just stand still. I feel his arms loosen around me, but he doesn't let go; it's as if he needs to be held as much as I need to hold him.

Jessie makes a little "ahem" sound.

Mark puts me at arm's length and checks me out. He says, "You look really cool," but he sounds sad and I wonder if my new look is a mistake, if he misses the old Molly with the ponytail and no eye shadow or lip gloss.

Jessie says, "You can thank me for that. Smoky brown is really her shade. And her new hairstyle? Totally my idea. Don't you think it articulates?"

Mark turns to her like he's in a stupor and asks, "Articulates?"

She raises her eyebrows. "Sorry. Forgot you're from Le Sueur. I should let you two catch up. It was nice to meet you, Mark."

Mark mumbles, "Nice to meet you, too."

Jessie says, "You guys have the cutest accents," before she closes the door softly behind her, like we're small children she's just put down for a nap.

Mark and I look at each other and I need his arms around me again so badly that I feel like an addict. Then I feel a little disoriented — this is the first time my Le Sueur life and my Columbia life have come together, and the experience is a bit surreal. It's as if they can't coexist.

Mark sits down on the bed, picks up Dante's *Divine Comedy*, flips through it. He says, "This looks hard."

"It is. How have you been?"

He puts the book back down. "Cool. Sorry to just show up. I know I should have called first."

I smile at him. "I'm just happy to see you." Suddenly, I remember the cut-out yearbook picture of him in its frame on my desk. I don't want him to think I'm a stalker. As he rubs his eyes I lean against my desk and, with one hand behind my back, quickly place the frame facedown.

He says, his eyes still shut, "Do you mind if I crash here tonight?"

I look at the single bed with him on it. I say shakily, "Sure." Then I say, "Of course." Then I say, "Sure," again.

He finally opens his eyes and says, "Cool."

"What are you doing in the city?"

"You know . . . errands and shit."

I wait for him to say more, but he doesn't. I ask him about his job, about New Jersey, about his parents, but all he does is grunt as he lies on his back, staring at the ceiling.

Finally, I ask him, "What's wrong?"

He rolls over, looks at me with those eyes. He says, "Nothing. Just wiped."

"Seriously, is something bothering you?"

He smiles at me, but it's a sad sort of smile, like he's in a receiving line at a wake. He says, "Really, I'm just wiped."

So I sit at my desk, trying to read, and Mark sits up on my bed, helping himself to some chips and a pop.

I think I've read the same line five times. It's like someone sprayed my brain with PAM: Nothing's sticking.

I hear the *crunch, crunch, crunch* of the potato chips, and then the *glug, glug, glug* sound he makes when he downs some pop. I return to the first line on the page, preparing to read it for the sixth time.

"Hey, Molly."

"Yes?"

"Mind if I take a shower?"

I turn and face him, see the potato chip crumb in the corner of his mouth. I say, "Just make sure you use the men's shower." I put together a personal hygiene kit for him: towel, soap, shampoo, toothbrush (my extra), toothpaste (Close-Up), and send him in the right direction. I tell him if any of the guys ask him why he's using their shower, he should say that he's my boyfriend.

By sheer force of will I make it through the entire chapter, though I couldn't tell you what happened. I set the book down, look at the clock, and am alarmed to find it's nearly three A.M.

There is no way I'm going to finish this book. I go online and get the gist of it, praying that will be enough.

When Mark returns, he's just wrapped in a towel, his wet hair clinging to his face and neck. He dumps his dirty clothes on the floor. I stare at his chest, which is smooth and flawless, dark brown from the long days outside painting. His nipples are the color of pennies.

He's not what you would call muscle-bound: He's wiry, his skin tight against his tall frame, the defined abs of his taut . . . *Jesus*, what am I thinking?

I turn away as he puts on his underwear. Next he flops onto the bed and curls up in the fetal position. When he's done, he says, "Don't worry, the light won't keep me up."

I say, "No, I need to get some sleep. I'll be right back."

I head to the women's shower with my towel and my makeup bag, a gift from Jessie. After a thorough shower (and I mean thorough), I shave my legs to the bikini zone. I brush my teeth and apply some deodorant. The final step is reapplication of eye shadow, lipstick, and just a bit of makeup to cover a zit that's forming on my chin. I put on my winter nightgown, the longest one I have, even though it's hot tonight.

By the time I get back to the room, Mark's asleep under a light sheet and it's four A.M. I groan softly as I try to position myself next to him on the bed. I have to be up in three and a half hours.

Mark wakes up a little and shifts to make room for me. I try to avoid contact with his bare chest and his bare legs and his bare arms, but it's not possible. When I find a position I can live with, he spoons me, sighing, "Good night."

Oh my God.

Fall asleep, Molly. Just fall asleep. You're tired, you can do it.

Think about boring things, like Mom watching her stupid television shows or Russ playing his stupid video games or Mark's strong arm around my midsection, just inches away from my . . . Oh my God.

Oh, good, my back's itchy.

I think my foot's about to cramp.

And then I hear what sounds like crying.

I sit up, turn on the light. "Mark?"

He wipes his eyes, embarrassed, and tries to pull himself together. "It's no biggie, Moll. Just turn out the light and let's go to sleep."

I run a hand through his hair, his thick, soft, silky hair. I desperately want to hold him, make it all better. I say, "Do you want to talk about it?"

He shakes his head. "It's nothing. I'm sorry I woke you up."

Part of me wants to comfort him, part of me can't bear removing my fingers from his hair. I want to brush away his tears, but I doubt he'd let me. I say, "It'll be okay."

He wipes his nose, and there's a hint of desperation in his voice as he says, "Let's go to sleep."

An hour or a year passes before Mark's breathing relaxes and I can tell that he's finally fallen asleep. I take the opportunity to move a little, try to ease the stiffness. I look at him in the darkness, his lips slightly parted now, as if he's waiting to be kissed.

When the alarm clock goes off, I finally release myself from Mark, who's ended up spooning me again. He mutters, "Hey," as I limp across the room to the desk, my leg asleep, the only part of my body that got any. As I turn off the alarm, I watch Mark close his eyes and stretch, the sheet down to his thighs, his thin, strong thighs. They're lighter in tone than his chest and arms, with just peach fuzz for hair. His abdomen rises and falls with each breath he takes. He sighs like an angel, and I admit that I feel lust — true, down-and-dirty lust. I want to kiss him hard, right on the lips. I think I could lose my virginity to him.

No, I'm certain of it.

I say, "How are you doing? Are you okay?"

He makes it plain that he doesn't want to talk about last night. He pretends to sleep.

So what do I do? Head to the women's shower with my wet towel and makeup kit. In the hall I run into Jessie, who looks clean, refreshed, together. She says, "Whoa, you look like hell!"

"And a good morning to you, too."

She says, "Sorry, sorry. Did you get any sleep at all?"

"No."

Her mouth's agape. "You mean you and Mark —"

"NO!"

"Well, you can't go on like this."

"I know. What am I going to do?"

Jessie puts a hand on my shoulder. "Make a pass at the guy. You're friends, right? Why not be friends with privileges?"

I rub my bloodshot eyes. "I don't want to be a friend with privileges."

"It may lead to something better."

"Or it may lead to total disaster."

She shakes her head. "You could do a lot worse than losing your virginity to Mark."

I nod, because I don't know what else to do.

OCTOBER

I spend the next few weeks completely and utterly confused and overwhelmed — confused by Mark, and overwhelmed by the sheer amount of reading and studying that is expected of me. One always complicates the other. When I want to think about Mark, I'm distracted by the stack of books on my desk that demand to be read (and understood, and analyzed, and regurgitated in class); when I try to study, I'm distracted by Mark, my beautiful Mark, who I've seen exactly twice since he spent the night: once for coffee (where he acted like nothing had happened), and once for lunch (where he acted like nothing had happened). Jessie is annoyed with him, saying he skipped the "sex with you" part and moved directly to the "pretending it never happened" part.

"After all," she says, "what's the point of pretending it never happened when it never did? He should at least have the common courtesy to give you something to feel awkward about."

As for Mark himself, he tries to keep things light and

casual, but there's always that look in his eyes, like he's a starving man holding a can of SpaghettiOs, but he doesn't have a can opener. I guess the word for his look would be *frustration*. I'm desperate to get him to talk about what's bothering him, but he insists that it's nothing. The Three *E*s have met several times to discuss the matter, but apart from Jessie telling me to make a pass at him and Lily cautioning me to let Mark take things at his own speed, we have come to no conclusions. Apart from the fact that I'm tired of taking things at Mark's speed. Why can't I set the pace? Why can't I, Molly Swain, post and enforce the speed limits?

Patience and understanding is hard when all you want to do is take him in your arms, squeeze him like a rag doll, and kiss him until his lips are swollen and raw.

Not that I would know what that's like.

Jessie (who I may have mentioned is from San Francisco) has decided it would be fun to go to a "queer" dance. She says we need to let loose around a group of hot guys who want nothing more from us than a dance. She also insists that gay guys dance better and are more fun than straight guys, but Lily thinks that's because there's no expectation of sex. Still, Lily agrees to go, saying we needed to blow off some steam. I need more to be convinced. I feel it won't be *culturally sensitive or appropriate* to crash a gay club just for the novelty of it. But Jessie insists we'll have an awesome time, and we can ask guys to dance without fear of rejection.

I need to practice my dance steps.

After our experience at Push Room, Jessie has decided we'll go to the 18+ night at a club in Hell's Kitchen called Exiles. We won't be able to drink, which is good for my budget and my health.

The place is full of guys and we're among the few females in the place. Frankly, I don't know what I expected, but I have to say the crowd, the setting, all of it, are a bit of a letdown. I was thinking it would be more shocking, or at least a bit more exotic. I don't know; Jessie's been to gay pride parades in San Francisco, and from her description I thought I'd see lesbian motorcycle gang members, men in chains, and an abundance of drag queens. We don't have drag queens in Le Sueur, although there are some women who could pass for men, probably because they've had too many children and work too hard.

At Exiles, the closest there is to drag queens are a few kids who just seem androgynous — guys who would make pretty girls and girls who would make really cute guys. Some in the crowd are dressed punk, some Goth, some prep, some casually in T-shirts and jeans.

Lily and Jessie are laughing and kidding around with a couple of guys who compliment Lily on her *fierce and amazing look.* As for me, I'm sucking on a diet Coke and pretending to enjoy myself.

Lily and Jessie are about to introduce me to their new friends, but I discreetly point between my legs, our signal that I have to pee (I drank my diet Coke too fast). I make it into a hall, which is lined with people, *gay and lesbian and bisexual and transgender and questioning and allied people* (according to a flier I was handed when we entered), and search for anything that resembles a bathroom.

There's an isolated little corridor I follow in the hopes that there's a bathroom at the end of it. My steps echo in the grimy hall and dim light that barely illuminates posters of musclemen who for some reason all have their arms behind their heads, displaying their armpits. I grow a bit concerned that maybe this wasn't such a good idea. Do people get mugged at 18+ *gay and lesbian and bisexual and transgender and questioning and allied people* nights? Jessie told me about fag bashers. They often come into gay clubs to scout out victims. And then there was that guy in Massachusetts who just pulled out a gun at a gay bar and started shooting.

That seems just about right. Straight Molly Swain from Le Sueur, Minnesota, is the victim of a hate crime at a gay club in Manhattan. I can see the *Le Sueur News Herald* now: *Homosexual Valedictorian in Coma, Alternative Lifestyle to Blame.* There would be a smaller article to accompany the feature: *Homosexual Valedictorian's Parents Mortified.*

Now I smell something, and in the shadows see the burning ember of a joint. (True, I don't smoke cigarettes or marijuana, but jeez, can you ever smell the difference.)

And then I just about drop dead.

"Mark?"

From behind his joint, Mark looks at me through the shadows. His eyes open wide.

All I can do is look at him.

What is he doing here?

Doesn't he realize this is a gay club?

I've got to get him out of here before he totally freaks out.

But before I can move, I hear him say, "Jesus, Molly, is that *you*?"

The joint falls to the floor as he hugs me tightly. He says, "Oh, dude, I knew it, I just *knew* it! You're gay!"

I'm what?

He kisses me on top of my head and pulls me back to take a good look at me. He says, "Jesus, for so long I thought I was the only one in Le Sueur!"

I gasp, "*You're gay?*"

And his expression changes from sheer delight to total panic. He lets go of me as he whispers, "*You're not?*"

I stare at him, like I'm seeing him for the very first time.

And we just stand there for a few centuries. When I find my voice, I ask him again. "You're gay?"

He just stares at me.

I say, "This is a gay club. You shouldn't be here." I point down the corridor to the dance floor and manage to say, before my voice cracks, "Those guys in there are gay. They'll think you're gay, too." We don't have gay clubs in Le Sueur. He mustn't realize . . .

He looks me in the eyes. He says, "Moll, I'm gay."

I shake my head. "No, you're not. Is this the cool thing to do now? Pretend you're gay?"

He looks away, saying, "No, it's not the cool thing to do now. It's who I am."

I turn away from him; I've got to find Lily and Jessie. I've got to get out of this place.

He grabs my arm, says, "Moll, wait."

"I have to go."

He begs, "Please, wait a minute."

So I stand there with his hand on my arm and I think about probability and how it had been working for me up until this very moment and how everything, the entire nature of existence, can change within a fraction of a second with a big bang that starts out small and then expands to the size of a universe, the one I find myself in right now, standing in the dank hall of a gay club with this other Mark, this *gay* Mark, this guy I thought I knew and knew I loved, and I wonder why this had to happen.

He says, "Can we talk?"

This other Mark wants to talk. The Mark I loved never wanted to talk, no matter how much I encouraged him to. But this other Mark wants to talk. I whisper, "Sure."

He nearly stutters as he tells me, "Nobody back home knows. Nobody back home can find out. Please, Moll, you can't tell anybody."

I say, "How long . . . ?"

"Since I was little. I've always known."

The pieces fall perfectly into place, and I realize that I'm a fool, probably the biggest idiot who ever lived. Of course he's gay. That's why he didn't go to the prom. That's why he wanted a secret identity like Spider-Man. That's why he couldn't wait to get out of Le Sueur. That's why he cried in my room. I hear Donna Piambino's voice again, *He's so out of your league.* Out of my league *and* gay. The little piece of hope I had that we might end up together has been stomped out. I'm such a loser I can't even have that.

He says, "Will you say something, Moll? Please?"

I can't help it, I actually laugh. "So you thought I was gay and I thought you were straight." But then I want to cry. "Didn't you know . . ."

"Know what?"

I blink too hard and say, "Nothing. It's not important."

He sounds desperate: "Moll, you gotta swear you won't tell anybody. It'll kill my parents."

I finally look at him and say, "I have to go."

He begs me now: "Please, Moll! You gotta keep this just between us!"

Now I feel the tears come and I shout, *"I have to go!"*

I run down the hall and onto the dance floor where guys dance with guys and girls dance with girls and I see Jessie and Lily dancing with each other, and the second they see me they rush over and put their arms around me and I start to cry, really cry, and I just never seem to run out of ways to humiliate myself.

They want to know what's wrong, but all I can say is, "I have to go home."

Lily says, "Let's go!"

The subway is crowded with people dressed for the clubs and workers heading to late shifts. I just sit, my head in my hands, as Lily and Jessie try to talk to me, desperate to know why I lost it at a gay club.

I mumble, "I don't want to talk about it."

Lily says, "Did some girl make a pass at you? Did that upset you?"

I groan, "Nobody made a pass at me." Then I add, "And no one ever will."

Jessie says, all sympathy, "Honey, did you *want* to meet a girl tonight? Is that what you're trying to tell us? 'Cause you know we'd be cool with it."

I sit straight up. "Why does everybody think I'm gay?! I'm in love with Mark!"

A guy in a security guard uniform reading the *Post* across the aisle looks over at us.

Lily asks, "Who thinks you're gay?" before adding, "Apart from Jessie, here?"

Jessie defends herself, saying, "I was just trying to be supportive."

I slump with a sigh. "Mark thinks I'm gay. Or he used to."

Now Lily asks, "Why would Mark think you're gay?"

The train comes to a stop, and people get on and off, including a young couple about my age, all dressed in black and white, who can't seem to keep their hands off each other. I look at them as they make out next to the security guard, and say, "Mark thinks I'm gay because he's gay."

I feel Lily's and Jessie's wide-eyed stares. Finally, Jessie says, "Why didn't you tell us this before?"

"I just found out. Tonight. At that club." And then the tears come again.

Lily says, "Ohmigod! Mark was *there*?"

The security guard slides down one seat to get away from the public display of affection. Over his head an advertisement asks WHO'S THE FATHER? BE CERTAIN WITH DNA TESTING FROM PREMIERE LAB. I say, "Mark was there."

"With a guy?" Jessie asks.

I wipe my eyes and snort a little to clear my nostrils. I don't know why I bother: This is New York, and a crying woman on a subway train is nothing out of the ordinary. I could be on fire and no one would bother to dump their double latte on me to put it out. I take a deep breath and say, "No, he wasn't with a guy. But he's gay. He told me so."

Jessie asks, "What did you say?"

I look at her. "I don't think I said anything. I'm not sure. I don't remember. I couldn't get away from him fast enough. I felt like I was going to throw up."

As the subway car rocks back and forth to its next destination, the Three *E*s sit in silence. When we make it back to JJ and my room with the picture of Mark in it, Jessie apologizes for thinking I might be gay and Lily says, "I know you're heartbroken, sweetie, but it's not Mark's fault, it's not your fault, it's nobody's fault."

I try to keep it together for their sake. "I know." I look at my answering machine, the light flashing. I've missed three calls, all of them, undoubtedly, from Mark.

Now Lily says, "Man, I didn't get *any* gay vibes from him. He's good at covering."

I lie on my bed and face the ceiling. "Tell me about it."

Jessie says, "Oh, I suspected."

Lily says, "Just because you're from San Francisco doesn't mean everyone is gay."

Lily's about to say something else, but I cut her off by telling them, "I'm wiped. I think I'll just go to sleep."

They make me promise we'll meet for coffee first thing in the morning. Then each of them leans down and gives me a hug. Once they're gone, I turn my head and stare at Mark's picture on my desk, the one where he's smiling, the one where the little gap in his teeth makes him all the more handsome.

The phone rings, but I don't answer. I don't know what to say.

I've hardly slept when the sun rises, so I give up on it altogether and listen to the messages on the answering machine.

Moll, it's me. Call me, please. We gotta talk. Promise me you won't tell anyone. Please, Moll, it's really important.

Yes, Mark, it is really important.

Moll, are you there? Pick up if you're there. Moll? I'm sorry you found out this way. I wanted to tell you that night I spent at your dorm. I thought you'd understand. Will you please call me when you get this? Please?

What difference would it have made if he told me that night he spent with me? I'd have made a complete fool of myself then instead of now. Like he would have told me anyway.

Moll, I just gotta know that you won't tell anybody. If you hate me 'cause I'm gay, fine, but Jesus, please don't tell anyone back in Le Sueur. Will you call me?

I listen to the next ones as I let the phone ring.

In a twisted sort of way, dreams really do come true. Mark can't stop calling me.

Over coffee, Lily and Jessie give me a pep talk. Lily says, "It's not Mark's fault he's into guys. He's just wired that way."

Jessie reminds me *yet again* that she's from San Francisco. "Gay guys are cool. They make really good friends. You should call Mark back, tell him you're his friend. I mean, this is what you wanted, right? To be his friend? Well, he could use one right about now."

Lily says, "Call him. The guy's scared shitless you're going to blow the whistle on him."

Jessie says, "Be a friend, Molly. You're not in the Valley of the Jolly Green Giant anymore."

What's only slightly more upsetting than Mark being gay is the fact that my two best friends in the entire world think I'm petty enough to make his life even harder than I know it must be. And that just because I'm from a small town I must be prejudiced. I say, "I'm just a little *disappointed*, okay? I *don't* hate gay people. I'm *not* a bigot. People from small towns aren't all bigots you know. I just wanted . . ."

As I start crying, Lily puts her arms around me and Jessie pats me on the back. I sob, "This is so stupid. There's no way he would have wanted me even if he was straight."

Jessie says, "You don't know that for a fact."

Lily says, "You never will."

I suppose that's some sort of comfort.

Lily and Jessie drop me off at my room with my promise that I will call Mark. I dial his number and when his aunt picks up, she says in her deep, dark voice, "Oh, yeah, he's been waiting for your call."

❖ ❖ ❖

And so Mark and I have arranged to meet for lunch at a Subway (the place to eat, not the place to catch a train) near Grand Central Station, his treat. The place is small and loud and crowded, and we sit at a table next to some men who argue in Spanish and then laugh loudly.

I look at my six-inch veggie and diet Coke as Mark says, his voice faltering, "Thanks again for meeting me."

I smile, nod.

He's worn just a single expression since I arrived, that of a small boy who's been caught doing something absolutely horrible. When I come up for a breath from the deep pool of self-pity I'm drowning in, I find myself wondering where he learned to be so ashamed of himself.

I say, "Mark, it's no big deal. I was just . . . surprised, is all. I had no idea." I mean that, I had no clue. None. Zip. *Nada.* Not even a single string of a notion.

Next I say, "Please don't worry. I'm cool with it." In other words, I lie. Not about the *not to worry* part, but about the *I'm cool with it* part. Replace *cool with it* with *heartbroken over it* and you'd be closer to the truth.

Looking at him across the little table from me is torture. Before I found out, it would have been the sort of torture that made me sadly excited and hopelessly hopeful. Now it's just torture.

Mark nods gently. When he can speak it's to say, "Thanks, Molly."

"You can stop thanking me now."

"Sorry."

We sit in silence for a while, listening to the men next to us laugh. At last Mark says, "You're always covering for me, Moll. First with chemistry, and now this."

"Just being a friend." What else can I be? There's no other option available.

More silence, at least from our table.

I ask, "Does anyone else know? From Le Sueur, I mean?"

Mark shakes his head. "Nobody. My folks are kinda religious. So's my aunt and uncle. They don't like gay people."

"They like you." I love you.

He looks at me directly, saying, "They don't know me."

"It might not be as bad as you think."

He looks at me as if I have no idea what I'm talking about. He says, "I got so lonely back home, you know? I know there are people at school and stuff who would have been cool with it, but I didn't feel like I could take a chance. Once one person knows, everybody knows."

"Well, I'm one person and I'm not going to tell anyone."

He says, "Talking about it helps. I don't really have any friends in New York yet. When I go to a club, I just hide in a corner. I mean, some guys have been nice, they ask me to dance and stuff, but I dunno, I just . . . don't know what to say. I mean, I *am* gay, but I don't understand how you're supposed to *be* gay."

Lily and Jessie told me to be a friend. Mom always says that if you love someone, you make sacrifices for them (here she was referring to my father). She says, *You love them unselfishly.* So I take a deep breath and I say, "Maybe we could go to a club together? You know, get you acclimated?" As soon as the words leave my lips, I know that watching him try to meet gay guys at a club is a very bad idea.

He looks at me, his eyes wide. "You mean it? You'd really come with me?"

Whatever regret I felt after making the offer vanishes when I look at his face, which has lit up like a Broadway marquee.

Lily and Jessie would be proud of me. Mom? I don't know, given the circumstances.

And still, I just want to lean over and kiss him.

Mark takes me up on my offer a week later. He arrives at my dorm room a full half hour early. He sheepishly says hello to Lily and Jessie, probably embarrassed by the fact that they know he's gay. When it's just the two of us, I have to say, "They're good people, Mark. They're not judging you."

He looks at himself in the mirror. "I know. It's just like . . . I feel like people won't take me seriously if they know I'm gay. Like I'm less than they are."

I look at him as he fine-tunes his hair. I say, "Don't talk to me about people not taking you seriously."

His reflection smiles at me. He says, "Thanks again for coming with me tonight. I don't like going out on my own."

I suppose that's a compliment, but the depressed part of me thinks he really means that *anyone will do.* I say, "I don't like going out on my own, either. But here I am, in New York, and it's worked out." In its own heartbreaking, joy-crushing, hope-annihilating way.

Now I wonder if this night out with Mark counts as my first date. If so, it's pretty pathetic. Even for me.

Mark decides that his hair is okay and looks at me with those sleepy eyes. "It just seems like when I go to a club, everybody else knows somebody or has somebody to talk to. And I just freeze when guys talk to me. I'm afraid I'll say something stupid."

Even though there's really no point, I put on some lipstick and check my look in the mirror before we head to the under-21 dance at the Gay and Lesbian and Bisexual and Transgender and Questioning and Allied and Whatever Else Center. Mark, of course, looks amazing. I, on the other hand, look like someone who only recently discovered that the boy she loves is gay.

At the Center we get our hands stamped and Mark leads me into the room where the dance is taking place. On the floor guys and girls move to the beat with confident, defiant expressions like they know we're watching them. I look at Mark as he looks at them. In Le Sueur he would saunter into a classroom like he didn't care what anyone thought of him, like it didn't make any difference, but here, tonight, he's timid, afraid, awkward.

He reminds me of me.

We watch in silence until he puts his mouth to my ear and says loudly enough so I can hear over the music, "It's like a different world. They're all so cool."

I say, "That's what I thought about Columbia kids, at first. Trust me, they wouldn't last two seconds in Le Sueur."

He laughs.

Then I say, because it's the truth, "Anyway, you're the hottest guy here. Don't let these city kids scare you. Just because they think they're better than us doesn't mean they are."

So we stand next to a wall drinking pop and staring at the people on the floor until a guy asks Mark if he wants to dance, and Mark blushes, looking at me. I smile (or as near to it as I can get) and nod slightly, like I'm giving him permission. This guy, whoever he is, holds out his hand like he's in some old movie, and Mark shyly takes it in his own. All I can do is watch as they make their way onto the floor where guys dance with guys and girls dance with girls.

I watch Mark and his partner as they move their bodies to the pulsating bass. Mark surprises me with his smooth moves, and I wonder if he practices when he's alone. As for Mark's partner — well, he can't take his eyes off Mark, which I find irritating. I mean, he must be thinking nasty thoughts about Mark, wondering what Mark looks like naked. For a nanosecond I picture the two of them together and just the idea of it makes me flinch.

Mark's partner is nice-looking but not in Mark's league. I scan the crowd for someone worthy of Mark, a handsome guy who won't undress Mark with his eyes. Near an exit I spot him, a tall guy in a tan button-down shirt and faded blue jeans. I like the cut of his dark hair, long, parted to one side, with some of it pushed behind an ear. He looks like a college student to me, maybe NYU. He looks like he's smart, someone with a good career ahead of him, someone who could take care of Mark. Once Mark's done with his current dance partner, I'll point out the tall guy with the hair.

This is what a supportive friend does. She points out the tall guy with the hair.

Even if it kills her.

The problem is that Mark's partner is monopolizing him. A slow dance starts, and the guy presses himself into Mark like I don't know what.

No one, not even a girl, asks *me* to dance.

Hours pass as I watch Mark switch partners as one guy cuts in on another. I don't understand why Mark was afraid to come on his own; these boys can't seem to get enough of him. Ultimately, Mark ends up with a guy who wears a shirt that's way too tight, showing off his muscles. I think I've been more than a sport leaning against a wall all night, so I interrupt them as they bounce around the floor to yet another techno beat.

I shout, "Hey, do you mind if we leave now? It's kind of late." Kind of late and boring and noisy. Who knew gay people could be so dull? Who knew I could be just as invisible at a gay dance as I am at a straight one? These people really should be nice to me. After all, I'm straight and not a bigot. They owe me.

Mark smiles and wipes some sweat from his forehead. "What?"

I shout louder this time: "You ready? 'Cause I'm ready to go."

The guy with pecs bigger than my breasts shouts, "You guys taking off?"

Mark shakes his head. "Come on, Moll, just a couple more dances?"

Tight Shirt says, "Don't worry, I'll take good care of him," and then he laughs like he just said something really funny, which, in fact, he did not.

"I'm *not* worried," I shout at Tight Shirt. "I'm just tired and ready to go."

Tight Shirt points to a pretty girl in jeans and a T-shirt who is standing by herself. "She looks nice. Why don't you ask her to dance?"

"I'm *not* gay!"

Tight Shirt says, "Oh," and winks at Mark.

Mark tells him, "Give me a second."

Mark pulls me off the floor and I already know what he's going to say, but he says it anyway. "Do you mind if I stay?"

Oh, sure, I can walk to the subway late at night by myself, get off at the 116th Street stop, and walk back to JJ alone. But he surprises me by having prepared for this little eventuality. He hands me some cash, saying, "Let's get you a cab."

Tight Shirt has joined us now, and Mark tells him, "We're just gonna grab Moll a cab. I'll be right back."

But Tight Shirt doesn't want to take any chances. "I'll go with you."

So we find ourselves out on the street with Tight Shirt pretending to be a gentleman by hailing me a cab. As I get in, Mark tells the driver to make sure I get inside my building before he drives away. To me, Mark says, "Thanks a lot for coming, Moll. I mean it, you're awesome."

My pleasure.

It's a long cab ride from the Village to Morningside Heights. All I can do is sit and stew, and I'm not really sure who I'm more mad at: Mark for ditching me, or myself for taking him there.

No, I'm mad that I'm still in love with him.

But then, this is what a good person does, she supports her friends, and she is sensitive to the hardships gay people face and she forgives them when they get carried away with their newfound freedom.

This is what a good person does.

But that doesn't mean I have to like it.

Mark pays me an impromptu visit the next day. When he shows up at JJ, he actually has hickeys, or "love bites" as my mom calls them. You can tell he hasn't slept because he has a crazy look in his eyes.

I say, "'Sup, Romeo? Spend the night in town?"

He looks embarrassed and doesn't say anything.

I ask, "Did you have fun, at least?"

He nods.

This is like a game of charades except he isn't acting out any clues for me. I lie: "That guy seemed nice."

He says, "Yeah, Jim's really cool."

And then he doesn't say anything at all. I ask, "So, why are you here?"

He says, "I needed to chill. It was like everyone on the subway knew. Like they were all looking at me. I didn't want to go back to my aunt and uncle's place." He's silent a moment before he says, "Can you tell when a person has . . . you know? Do I look different?"

I smile politely, not wanting to hear the details. I say, "You and this Jim guy . . . ?"

Mark blushes. "No, we didn't go all the way. But pretty close. I've never made out with a guy before."

I sigh. "No one can tell by looking at you, Mark."

Now Mark gushes, "I've never made out with a guy before. It was so awesome. I don't know how people go to classes or to their jobs or anything. I just wanna make out all the time, twenty-four hours a day, seven days a week."

So I guess this is what requited love — or requited lust, anyway — looks like.

And it's not for the squeamish.

Now he says, "Man, you are so lucky to be a girl. You make out with guys and nobody cares! If I were you I would've made out all the time in high school, I mean *all* the time. Do you know how many dudes I wanted to make out with back in Le Sueur? All those parties I went to where everyone was making out but me, until I finally had to stop going? I mean, Jesus, when I think of all the time I've wasted."

If I had any lingering doubts, they're gone: Gay guys and straight guys may be attracted to opposite sexes, but at the end of the day, they're *all* guys.

Mark says, "Who did you make out with in high school?"

"I forget."

"Come on, you don't forget something like that. Was it weird when he stuck his tongue in your mouth? 'Cause at first it felt weird, but then, wow, I mean, dude, it was like, wow!" He keeps talking about making out, but then he's quiet. He looks at me, astonished. Seriously now, he asks, "You *have* made out, right?"

"No, Mark. Out of the two of us, you're the only one who has made out. *Happy?*"

"Dude, we gotta find you somebody. You don't know what you're missing."

NOVEMBER

Weeks pass and the only time I hear from Mark is when he and his *boyfriend* have had a fight. When I complained to Lily, she just shakes her head, saying, "This is what people do when they fall in love. They only call you when something goes wrong. Don't worry, once he's over that love-makes-you-stupid phase, you'll have your friend back."

The empty answering machine in my dorm room lets me know that things are going well for Mark. I should be happy for him.

Today is my phys ed class, which has turned out to be one of my favorites, thanks to the fact that I don't have to try and make sense of Virginia Woolf in order to participate. (Bet she wouldn't have passed Columbia's swimming test, so why do we have to read her?) Once I've changed into my workout clothes (basically a burka made out of sweatsuit material), I join my classmates who are already warming up and working the machines and free weights. I've gone from just being able to press the bar itself to adding some thirty pounds in weights. One of the other students always spots me when I press, just in case my arms fail. He's someone I noticed my first day in class, a guy who looks as intense as Mark looks lost. His name is Simon, and, like me, he's going to study physics.

He's standing behind me as I lie on the bench, my arms gripping the bar suspended above me. He says, "How many?"

I say, "I think I'm going to go for seven or eight."

"Need a lift off?"

"No, I'm good."

I inhale deeply and lift the bar up and position it over me. I inhale on the descent, I exhale loudly on the quick ascent.

"Good form," Simon tells me.

I make it to six and start to struggle. Simon says, "Come on, Swain, you can do it. Give me two more."

On seven I'm bright red and my arms are failing on the ascent. Simon says, "Push, push, push! Come on!"

I make it to seven, but just barely.

"Not bad," he tells me. "Soon you'll be the She-Hulk."

Did I mention how many physics majors are comic book geeks? I smile and look at him. He's more cute than handsome. Well, not cute, but not ugly, either. If he let his brown hair grow a bit longer, it would make him look a bit better since his ears stick out, just a little. And his lips are little crooked and his mouth a bit small, but his skin is clear and his brown eyes are sleek. And his eyebrows are pretty dramatic, I must say.

But most important, he's going to be a physics major.

If I were a mad scientist, I would put Simon's brain in Mark's body. Then I would program the heart to beat for nobody but me.

"Everything okay, Swain?" Simon asks me.

I pat my face with a towel. "Fine, why do you ask?"

"You're staring at me."

I smile. "Am I? Just spacing out, I guess. Thanks for the spot."

"No problem," he tells me before he walks over to the pec deck, a favorite machine of both guys and girls who are eager to increase their chest size.

And so the day goes by with me considering the possibility of pursuing someone new to get my mind off Mark. After a couple of hours in the library catching up on my reading, I return to JJ to discover the man himself waiting for me in the lobby. He looks upset.

"Mark?"

He looks up at me shyly, says, "Jim and I had a fight. Mind if I crash here tonight?"

Jim. The Boyfriend. I say, "Not a problem," a little too easily. Why does him having a fight with the Boyfriend give me pleasure?

He gets up, gives me a hug. "I left a message for him with your number so maybe you won't be stuck with me tonight. If he calls to apologize, I mean."

I repeat: "It's not a problem."

So Mark hangs out in my room as I shower, shampoo, shave, and re-apply makeup so I can go to bed. You'd think I wouldn't bother with all that now that Mark is gay, gay, gay, but oh well.

He's in his briefs and nothing else when I get back to the room. He says, "Hope I don't keep you up. It's hard for me to fall asleep when I'm upset."

I position myself next to him, let him spoon me as he says by way of good night, "You're a good friend, Molly. Thank you."

I mutter, "Sweet dreams," and feel his arm around my waist. I imagine a parallel universe where I turn around, kiss him hard on the lips, and he kisses me back. But in my own universe, I try to content myself with the knowledge that I am indeed a good friend.

It's that thought I doze off to, so tired that even sharing the bed with Mark isn't enough to keep me up.

I'm dreaming about Brian Greene, eleven dimensions (in each one Mark is gay), and spotting Virginia Woolf as she bench-presses *a barbell of one's own* when the phone rings. Before I can even open my eyes, Mark climbs over me to answer it.

I hear him say to the receiver, "Jim?"

Then I hear, "Oh."

Then I hear, "This is Mark. . . . Yeah, I was Molly's lab partner."

Then I hear, "Oh . . . okay . . . I'll tell her."

I look at him in the darkness, confused. He says, "Your mother doesn't want to *disturb* you. She'll call back. Um, she's pretty pissed, Moll."

I stare at the ceiling, say, "Great. Why did you answer the phone?"

"I thought it might be Jim."

"Did she say why she's calling so late?"

"Your brother just came home high as a kite."

"Great. Just great. And now, on top of that, she thinks I'm a slut."

Mark climbs back into bed, apologizing. Then he says, "She'll get over it."

He puts his arm around my waist but I push it away as I say, "I'll just tell her the truth."

He tenses up. "What do you mean?"

"That's you're gay and it's no big —"

Mark grabs my arm. "You can't tell her that! It'll be all over town!"

I look at him, incredulous. "You want her to go on thinking what she's thinking?"

Before he can answer, the phone rings again. We both stare at it like it's a bomb about to go off. Mark says, "You should get that."

I say, "No way. *You* can answer it."

"We can just let it ring."

I grunt as I get off the bed. "Oh no, let me. I can hardly wait to explain you to my mom. You *know* she'll assume I'm pregnant, just like she was when she was my age." I pick up and offer a tentative "Hello?"

It's a guy on the other end of the line, young, smug, undoubtedly wearing a tight shirt to highlight his pecs. He says coolly, "Hey, is Mark there?"

I sigh. "Let me see if he's home at present. One moment, please." I cover the mouthpiece and say to Mark, "It's the makeout king of Greenwich Village."

Mark practically rips the phone out of my hands. "Hey!" he shouts, too enthusiastically, and I know he's infatuated and obsessed with this guy, and he probably thinks it's love. As he talks softly into the phone, like a pigeon cooing, I curl up in the fetal position on the bed and put a pillow over my head.

What am I going to say to Mom?

The next day, the Three *E*s hold an emergency summit at Café 212 on the issue of mothers and daughters, specifically me and my mom. Jessie and Lily are of one mind, that I should tell Mom that Mark is gay. I explain Mark's reasons for not wanting me to. Le Sueur is a small town and it's hard to keep your business private. But Jessie's insistent, telling me that "mothers can handle fag hags for daughters. But it's hard for them to accept that their daughter is sleeping with guys."

Lily says to Jessie, "I thought you said your mom was cool."

Jessie says, "About other people's kids. When it

comes to me, well, let's just say she's got that old-timey religion. I still haven't told her about Chris."

Chris is Jessie's new boyfriend. She met him on the subway when they both got off at 116th. He's handsome, friendly, wealthy, and this is his last year at Columbia. Lily and I have privately decided that he's using Jessie for what Lily calls *barely legal sex*, since Jessie graduated high school early and only turned eighteen a few weeks ago.

Lily picks at a muffin, popping a few crumbs into her mouth. "Mark's putting you in an unfair position. Why should *you* be the one in the closet, pretending he's your boyfriend?"

I nod, I know, I know. Why should I upset my mom so much to protect Mark? I say, "I just feel like this is all my fault. I was the one who said he could spend the night in my room. I can't out him to my mother."

Lily and Jessie look at each other meaningfully. Jessie says, "You were doing him a favor. Now it's his turn to do you one. If you think your mom can keep her mouth shut about Mark, why not tell her? Yeah, she's still going to be mad, but at least she won't have to worry about you sleeping with a real guy."

Lily says, "Mark's a real guy."

Jessie says, "You know what I mean."

I stare at my cup of regular coffee with the skim milk and Sweet'n Low. I say, "I think I can trust my mom with this. It isn't like she hasn't kept secrets herself."

Lily says, "What secrets?"

I say, "Me. Anyone who can do the math knows she was pregnant when she got married, but she still insists I was conceived on their honeymoon."

Jessie says, "I call that leverage."

Lily says, "I call that untouchable. If you think she can keep a secret, trust that. Don't bring her own past into it."

I take a deep breath, pull out my calling card, and dial. After a few rings, Russ picks up. When he hears my voice, he shouts, "Molly-Pop! 'Sup??"

I tell him the latest news about my classes, but he's mostly interested in strength training and asks me if I'm buff and cut and ripped. When I ask him about school he mumbles something about it being boring as hell, and before I can say anything else he hollers for Mom, knowing that the minutes on my calling card are precious commodities or afraid that I'll bring up the fact that he came home stoned.

Mom offers me a cryptic, "Hello."

I squeak out, "Hi, Mom."

And then there is The Silence. Trust me, I have only been in trouble a very few times compared to my brother, but I recognize The Silence. It's as loud as fireworks on the Fourth of July.

I say, trying to break the tension, "Mark sends his love."

She says, "Very funny. He sounded well when I spoke to him. I just didn't expect him to sound well *from your dorm room at two in the morning.*"

Actually, it was three in the morning Eastern Standard Time, but I don't correct her. I close my eyes. "I'm sorry."

And then she starts: "I mean, Jesus Christ, Molly. Jesus Christ!"

Mom is a lot like Dad when she's angry, only she doesn't get angry as often as he does. I say again, "I'm sorry."

"There's sorry as in confession, and then there's sorry as in you've been caught in the act. You tell me which one is the most sincere."

I make a little joke: "Caught in the act?"

"Molly, you're just a kid. I swear to God, if you throw away your education for some boy —"

"He's gay."

Silence again, but not The Silence. After a moment or two, she asks quietly, "He's what?"

I repeat myself: "He's gay." Forgive me, Mark. "He's a homosexual. There's nothing going on between us. We're friends."

The Silence again.

I offer, "I know it was a stupid thing to do, but I just felt sorry for him, you know, because he's different."

"I see." A long pause. "And you're in love with him."

"Mom!"

She gives me her don't-talk-back-to-me voice. "Molly, you were mooning over that guy all last year. *Mark-my-lab-partner this* and *Mark-my-lab-partner that.* And now this. You in New York, having sleepovers with a homosexual you're in love with!"

Maybe it's the fact that I can't see her that makes me bold. "Excuse me! I was being a friend to someone who needed one! It's not like he got me pregnant and we had to —"

"You tread cautiously, young lady."

"I'm just saying he's a friend. And promise me you won't tell anyone, not even Dad, that he's gay."

"Why not?"

"His parents will freak out."

Mom makes a little "hmmph" noise before she says, "All right. I won't say a word. But Molly, this is a bad idea. You're in love with him, and he can't return that love, at least in the way you want. This is a train wreck waiting to happen."

I insist: "I love him, but I'm not in love with him. There's a difference."

She says, "You may try to convince yourself that's true, but you can't convince me."

I gasp, "Why not?"

She says, "Because I can hear it in your voice."

In my strength training class the next day, Simon remarks on my more-vigorous-than-usual workout. "Are you taking steroids or what?"

I grunt as I lift the barbell back into position. "Just working off some frustration."

He nods, says, "Remind me never to get you frustrated with me."

I get up off the bench, put my hands on my hips, and blow a stream of air out of my lungs like cigarette smoke. I look at him matter-of-factly, say, "Deal."

He takes my weights off the bar, replaces them with

heavier ones. When he's done, he lies back on the bench press and says, "Spot me?"

I hesitate; he usually has a guy spot him. I say, "I can't lift that much."

He says, "Between the two of us, I'll be fine."

"Okay," I say, unconvinced. "How many reps?"

He says, "Twelve."

I watch him nervously, parroting the encouragement I hear other guys offer one another. "Push, you got it. It's all you."

To my immense relief, he does all twelve unassisted. He sits up, panting. "Cool. Just let me rest a minute, and then we'll do twelve more."

As he catches his breath, I say, "Any Greene sightings?" I mean Brian Greene, the professor I came here to study with.

Simon says, "No, not yet." Then he adds, after a moment or two, "You want to go see *Cosmic Collisions*? There's a special encore showing this Friday at the Hayden Planetarium."

Did he just ask me out?

On a date?

I fight the temptation to ask him if he just asked me out. I tell myself, *Don't ask for clarification, Molly. Just say* yes, *like this happens to you all the time.* I try to act nonchalant as I say, "Cool."

He lies back down. "There's a Vietnamese place there where we could grab something to eat before the show. How 'bout I come get you around five?"

"Cool," I repeat. What I want to do is scream: *A guy has finally asked me out!* But if Lily and Jessie have taught me anything, it's not to show how desperate you feel. Lily has a term for it: *chick poker.* Even if you've been sacrificing children and small animals at midnight to get a guy to ask you out, play it cool when he finally does.

He does another set, but starts to fail at ten. I squat and place my hands next to his on the bar as I even out his lift and assist him on the ascent.

He thanks me for spotting him.

When I get back to my room I call Mark, who is actually at home. When he asks what Simon looks like, I lie, just a little bit. Mark says, "He sounds *hot.*"

At the dining hall, the Three *E*s meet to discuss Chris, Jessie's boyfriend, who has not been returning her calls.

Understandably, Jessie is somewhat sullen. And Lily is a bit disappointed in herself; she's started going out with a white guy. "I'm not a racist," she tells us, "it's just such a stereotype. Asian girl with white guy. I don't want my Asian brothers to think they're second best."

Jessie says, "I wonder if something's wrong."

I look at her, confused. I say, "What do you mean?"

Jessie says, "Maybe something's happened, and that's why Chris hasn't called me. You know, like a crisis or something."

Lily says, "You've left messages; he knows how to get ahold of you."

Jessie nods and contemplates her plate.

Lily says, "You know what we need? A sistuh-woman-sistuh night out. We need to slap on a coat of primer and hit the town."

I mutter, "I don't know."

Jessie says, "Has anyone ever told you that you remind them of Eeyore?"

Okay, fine. I say, in uncharacteristically un-Eeyore-like fashion: "You know what? Lily, you're right. Sitting around moping about AWOL boyfriends and gay men is a waste of time. Let's do a girls' night out."

Jessie lifts her head up, says, "I'm in. If we go out Friday. I want to save Saturday in case Chris calls."

I say, suddenly meek, "I can't on Friday. I have a date."

Their jaws drop to the floor, which I find insulting. "I didn't say I discovered a cure for cancer. I said I have a date."

They're thrilled for me, a bit *too* thrilled if you ask me. It's like I'd been given the last rites and had my breathing tube removed, only for them to discover that I can inhale and exhale all on my own.

Lily: "What's his name?"

"Simon."

Jessie: "What's he look like?"

"He's nice-looking."

Lily: "What's his major?"

"Physics."

They look at each other knowingly. My nice-looking date who majors in physics is clearly a nerd.

Mark decides to stand on his head. He had a fight with his uncle who accused him of *tomcatting around instead of working* (they paint indoors fall and winter) so he showed up to hang out in my room until it's time for his date with Jim.

Anyway, Mark's feet are pressed against a wall, and all the blood's rushing to his head.

"That's *so* hot," I tell him as his face grows pink.

He drops back down to a kneeling position. "Moll, I'm gonna lose my mind if I keep living with my aunt and uncle. And the paint fumes are frying my brain. I've got to get a new job and a place of my own in the city."

"I'm sorry," I say as I take a second look in the mirror.

Mark says, "So tell me more about your date."

I give up on my eyes. "He's a nice guy. He's from Long Island, he's Jewish, he's nineteen, and he commutes to campus."

I know what's coming next.

"And he's hot, right? You told me he can press two seventy-five."

This was an exaggeration. Now I say, "He's so hot that, compared to him, the sun's an iceberg."

"Dude, for real?"

I resent the fact that he doesn't believe me. I say, "He's very nice. Is there anything wrong with being very nice?"

"*Nada,* Moll."

There's a knock on the door. Mark and I look at each other. I squint out the peephole. There's Simon, in jeans and a sweater, some *product* in his hair. I open the door and he says, "Hey, you ready?" Then, noticing that I'm not in my workout burka, he says, "You look nice."

"Thanks," I say as I take his hand and lead him into the room. "Simon, this is my friend, Mark. Mark, Simon."

Simon looks at Mark, a confused expression on his face. Mark looks Simon up and down, weighing and measuring him on the gay guy's *hot* scale. Cautiously, Simon says, "Nice to meet you."

Mark offers his usual "'Sup?"

I make a point of asking Mark, "You and your boy-friend going out tonight?"

He blushes, then says quietly, "I already told you we were."

I'll apologize to Mark later — for what, I'm not exactly sure.

Simon shakes Mark's hand and tells him to have a good night. Then we're off. We take a packed 1 train downtown to 79th Street. Simon says, "Why was that guy hanging out in your room?"

"He's squatting."

"What do you mean?"

I say, "He's there a lot. He lives out in Montclair and needs a place to hang in the city."

Simon asks stiffly, "Do you hang out with a lot of gay guys?"

I say, "Just him."

"How do you know each other?"

"Oh, *that's* a long story."

We exit the subway and emerge into the cool evening. It only takes us a few blocks to get to Café Phó. As we sit at our table, Simon complains about living at home, the long commute from Long Island to Morningside Heights, and his parents who are worried that their grandchildren won't be Jewish. "My parents push me to date Jewish girls. They always say, 'Just a suggestion,' but you know it's more than that. And they're already talking about grandchildren. I'm only nineteen."

"Oh. Well, my parents are in no rush for grandkids. Not with my brother acting like a two-year-old most days. And as for religion, we're Christmas-and-Easter Catholics."

He smiles, looks at me sweetly. "Are there any Jews in Le Sueur?"

"Of course," I say, trying to think of who they might be. "We always have a Jewish senator representing

Minnesota, too. There was Boshwitz, and then Wellstone, and then Coleman."

He looks at the menu. "That's nice. I always heard Minnesota was a progressive state."

"Actually, Boshwitz and Coleman are Republicans."

He frowns.

I look at the menu, but the dishes aren't exactly what they serve at Boss Burger or the Caribou Gun Club. "What do you recommend?"

"Are you a virgin?"

I blush and say, "Yes. Is that a problem for you? I know some guys won't date virgins."

Now *he* blushes. "That was my lame attempt at being hip. I just meant, is this your first time at a Vietnamese restaurant?"

I nod, mortified.

He says, "I think it's cool you're a virgin. Are you going to wait until you're married?"

I stammer, "That's the plan." Well, for now, anyway.

He looks at me as if he's carefully weighing something in his mind, calculating the odds. Then he smiles and nods approvingly. "Good for you."

I'm relieved by his reaction but anxious to change the subject. "What should I order?"

He says matter-of-factly, "Leave the ordering to me.

We always ate Chinese or Vietnamese on Christmas when I was growing up."

Over spring rolls, Simon stops talking about anything personal; mostly he wants to talk about string theory and M theory. He says, "Imagine it, Molly — our generation will be the one to demonstrate that matrix theory is real, true. I think it will herald a wonderful new age of discovery and enlightenment. Reality will be redefined!"

"So you're a matrix man?"

He raises his eyebrows in disbelief. "Is your pope Catholic?"

"Why matrix theory?"

He says, "It brings it all together: strings, branes, space, and time. All composed of zero-branes."

"There's still a lot of work to be done. As they say, *the math is hard.*"

His eyes light up. "That's what I'm saying — in our lifetime matrix theory will be validated. It's a new renaissance for physicists. It's all coming together, relativity, quantum mechanics, everything."

I take a sip of tea. "Does it ever overwhelm you? That we only glimpse a tiny bit of reality?"

"Overwhelm? No. I think we only perceive as

many dimensions as we're equipped to, and that's not necessarily a bad thing. Does it depress me that we can only comprehend up and down, back and forth, and the passage of time? Yes. But then, everything depresses me. My mom says I'm *morose*."

I say, "What's there to be morose about?"

He says, "What isn't there to be morose about? The war, global warming, overpopulation, mass extinctions, religious fanaticism, my parents."

I look at him.

"That last thing on the list was my attempt at a joke."

I smile. Simon is more than meets the eye. I say, "I was valedictorian at my high school and my address was about global warming. If I think about it too much, I get *really* depressed."

He looks right at me with his dark, glistening eyes and says with a grin, "You know, I've been looking for someone who gets depressed over the same things that I do."

I laugh and look away; his brown eyes are just too intense.

I get back to JJ early. I had wanted to go out for coffee after the movie, but Simon had to get back to Long Island, and he was feeling tired. So I curl up in bed with some essays I have to read and respond to by next week for University Writing. I'll admit, I was waiting for Simon to hold my hand, but perhaps *Cosmic Collisions* isn't the right film for that sort of thing.

In any event, all Simon said was that he had a good time and that he would see me in strength training.

I hear the Two *E*s laughing in the hallway. They pound on my door before they open it, then fall into my room.

Jessie crisscrosses to the closet, opens the closet door, and says dramatically, "Hi, Mark!"

"Very funny," I say.

Lily says, "It wasn't the same without you, Molly. I mean, we still got drunk, but it wasn't the same."

The phone rings and it's Mom. Molly and Jessie laugh as we talk. I tell Mom, "It's pretty late for you to be calling."

Mom hears Molly and Jessie and says, "Are you having a party in your room?"

"Just some friends. What's wrong?"

"In case you haven't noticed, we haven't spoken for a while, Molly. I was going to wait for you to call me, but now I've given up. How are you?"

"Fine."

"And how is Mark?"

"Fine."

"Well, since everyone's fine, I guess I'll say good-bye."

I say, "Mom, guess what? I went on a date tonight. I think."

And we patch things up as Mom quizzes me about *the new man in my life.*

By nine the next morning, I'm in Lily's room and we've had three little pots of black coffee with no cream or sugar. She calls her small automatic coffeemaker the Last Refuge of the Damned, only to be used when nothing else is available or she can't bring herself to leave her room. Lily says she doesn't have a hangover, but she's taken four aspirin in the last two hours. Jessie finds us brewing a fourth pot when she wanders in, asking if she can have some, too. She looks worse off than Lily.

Jessie says, "God, my head. Why do I keep teaching myself the same lesson?"

Lily says, "Because we're idiots. With each martini we think we're funnier and hotter and having more fun than we actually are. And then the morning comes along and kicks us in the ass."

Jessie sighs, "If there was only a way to get drunk and not have a hangover."

Lily says, "Yeah, *that* would be healthy." Then, to me she adds, "Oh my God, I forgot to ask! How was your date?"

I stare at my cup of black, filmy coffee. "Fun. We ate Vietnamese and the film was really good."

Jessie asks, "You make out?"

I say, "No."

Lily asks, "Good-night kiss?"

I shake my head. "No. I guess he just asked me out as a friend. Or maybe he really was freaked out by the fact that I'm a virgin."

Lily is aghast. "How did that come up in the conversation?"

I say, "Me being stupid, that's how. Anyway, I think he just wants to be friends."

Jessie says, "Don't you just love it when the guy you're interested in wants to be your *friend*? The guy I was in love with in high school said we should just be friends. I told him I had plenty of friends, and when one of them died, I'd give him a call."

This doesn't make me feel much better.

At the next strength training class, I *think* that Simon is flirting, but since no one has ever really flirted with me before, it's hard to say. He's rolled up his short sleeves to show off his upper arms, which are very impressive when pumped up, and after we spot each other on the bench press, he shadows me as I work the circuit. I'm flattered, but at the same time some of the machines don't make me look my best; the leg press I'm on right now makes my butt look big.

Simon says, "I had fun the other night. I don't get out much, just spend my time commuting or studying."

I grunt as I push up with my legs.

He says, "Exhale on the lift."

I nod, my face turning red from the exertion. I put on too much weight in an effort to impress Simon. Now he's saying, "Don't rush on the descent; it's more important than the push."

I smile, wishing he would move on until I'm done with the leg press. He folds his arms across his chest and spreads his legs apart and rocks back and forth, coaching me as I do my reps. His cargo shorts go all the way down to his knees and, from what I can see of his legs, they're a bit too hairy.

I struggle with the final rep. He claps his hands together, says, "Push, come on, Molly, you can do it!"

And I do it.

I can finally stand up and not be pointing my big butt at him. When we reach the pec deck, I tell him to go first, I could use a breather. I watch him as he does his reps, watch his chest rise and fall as he closes his sleek eyes and opens them again.

He finishes, and with a gasp, asks, "You want to hang out this weekend? I don't know, a movie or something?"

Play it cool, Molly. I smile, say, "That'd be fun."

He says, "Or maybe you want to do something touristy, like see a show on Broadway or go to a museum."

Play it cool, Molly. I say, "That'd be fun."

He stands, wipes his face with a towel. "So . . . what do you want to do?"

Play it cool, Molly. I say, "Your choice."

"No, really, I want you to choose."

I say, "It all sounds good to me." Then I notice him growing irritated by my inability to make a simple decision. "But probably a movie." This seems the best choice; we can be together without having to make small talk. Then after the movie we can talk about the movie.

Why is it the more I like a guy the harder it is to talk to him? There must be a mathematical equation or graph to explain this perverse relationship, e.g.:

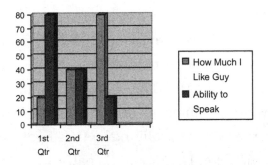

When class is over, Simon tells me he'll pick me up at JJ Friday night. All I have to do is choose a movie. Back at JJ, I call Mark to let him know about the second date, that he's not the *only* one in New York with a love life, but his aunt tells me he's on a job.

So I sit on my bed, trying to pick a movie.

❖ ❖ ❖

When Simon shows up at my room on Friday night, he looks really good, in a long-sleeve blue dress shirt with cargo pants and hiking boots. He's gotten a haircut, though I wish he would let it grow out to cover his ears a bit. Still, he looks wonderful. He presents me with a small gift, a copy of *Equations of Eternity: Speculations on Consciousness, Meaning, and the Mathematical Rules That Orchestrate the Cosmos* by David Darling.

I skim it excitedly. "Looks great!"

"He's an astronomer, not a physicist, but it's still a good book." Simon looks around before he asks, "So where's your squatter today?"

"Looking for Mr. Right, I guess." Just like me.

I wait for Simon to notice my new outfit (bought with money I don't really have) that I got especially for our movie date. I clear my throat a little in the hopes he'll comment, but all he says is, "We'd better get going, the theater's a hike."

Finally, on the subway heading downtown, he looks at me sitting next to him and says, "You look very nice."

"Thanks," I say.

In an effort to get to know him better, I try to engage him in something other than quantum theory, but it proves difficult. For example, when I bring up politics, he says, "You know what Einstein said: 'Equations are more important to me, because politics is for the present, but an equation is something for eternity.'"

When I talk about how inspiring the Manhattan skyline is, he says, "And it only exists as a material reality at the instant of observation."

An observer of this date would probably hypothesize that it will not go well.

At the theater, a small place in need of maintenance, we have our choice of seats. Simon selects two right in the middle. As we settle in, he says, "You're sure this movie's good? There's only three other people here."

I mimic Lily, "It's won a lot of independent film awards. Thought-provoking, sentimental, yet without sentimentality."

Simon smiles. "I see."

The lights dim and the movie begins right away. I plan to make a note of the scene where Simon puts his arm around me. According to Lily, the *arm-around-the-date-inducing-scene* will tell you a lot about a guy and what moves him. Some guys put their arm around you after a good laugh, others during a tragic scene, while others choose the frightening scene. Lily's theory is that good-laugh-scene guys are fun but don't want to get serious, tragic-scene guys are sensitive and high maintenance, and frightening-scene guys are opportunistic. Lily says I want a sentimental-scene guy.

The film is in black and white, and seems to have been shot with a hand-held camera. An old man in a dress approaches the camera, but when he comes closer, we discover he actually is a bald old woman. She looks dramatically into the camera and says, in a frightened whisper, "*Een ogenblikje alstublieft!*" The subtitles tell us she's saying *One moment please!*

For the next hour she approaches strangers on the street, saying, *Een ogenblikje alstublieft!* From there we follow each stranger's tragic end: One gets hit by a car, another has a heart attack, a third has a girder fall from the sky and land on top of her, a fourth simply starts crying and can't stop.

All without any other dialogue.

And then the movie just *keeps* going.

From the speakers we hear "*Een ogenblikje alstublieft!*" every few minutes as I glance at Simon, horrified. What could Lily have been thinking? Simon feels me watching him and he returns my gaze with a look of *What the f———?* on his face. He whispers, "Well, you're right — no one can accuse it of sentimentality."

I whisper, "I'm so sorry; it got great reviews."

"*Een ogenblikje alstublieft!*"

Simon asks, "From who?"

A woman two rows behind us hisses what sounds like "*How up or!*" I guess she wants us to be quiet.

Simon says, "I need to stretch my legs. Do you want something from the lobby? A soda or something?"

"*Een ogenblikje alstublieft!*"

I say, "We don't have to stay." On the screen a child in a wheelchair spontaneously combusts.

Simon says, "There has to be a point to all this. Let's see it through."

"*Een ogenblikje alstublieft!*"

And so time crawls by and what should have been a wonderful first date film has a surreal body count that I've lost track of. Finally (and I mean finally), the film ends with the old woman staring into the camera and asking "*Een ogenblikje? JA! EEN OGENBLIKJE!*" before breaking into five minutes of manic laughter.

And then the credits roll.

The film not only kills our appetites, it also gives us *nothing* to discuss afterward, save how awful it was. Now I'm worried that Simon will never ask me out again. When he drops me off at JJ, he gives me a little kiss, but I can't tell if it was a shy first kiss or a kiss-off.

The next day Lily realizes her mistake. It was a different Dutch film she wanted us to see.

The next few days, Simon doesn't call, but I remain hopeful he still may phone me at any *ogenblikje.*

It's Thanksgiving. Mom called to wish me a Happy Turkey Day and to get the latest on Simon, but unfortunately, there isn't much to tell. Dad's working because he gets paid more on holidays. So Mom and Russ are going over to Aunt Betty's for dinner.

As for me, I'm having a real home-cooked meal with Mark, his aunt and uncle, and his cousin and her family.

Mark is a gentleman and picks me up in his uncle's car. On the ride out he reminds me at least a dozen times that, for our dinner, he's straight and I'm his girlfriend. He asks me if I think I can convincingly play the role of the girlfriend.

I say I'll do my best.

The uncle and cousin seem nice, but the aunt is a bit of a shock. With her hair dyed bright red, she looks like Ronald McDonald's post-menopausal sister. Who has let herself go.

And the craggy voice she uses on the phone is even louder and more guttural in person.

So here I am, sitting in the *media room* with Mark, his uncle, and his cousin's husband, watching football. The cousin's husband is a friendly guy in his late twenties and the uncle drinks beer and flirts with me during the commercials. The aunt's in the kitchen with her daughter, and I have a vague suspicion that I'm supposed to be in there with them.

During a break in the game, the uncle asks me, "So you're from Le Sueur, too?"

"That's right."

"Only been there once myself for the in-laws' family reunion. Kind of a quiet place." He points at Mark and asks me, "And you two were an item in high school?"

Mark mutters, "Uncle Rob, come on. . . ."

I get up and say, "I should help in the kitchen."

But Mark's uncle shoots Mark a look before he says to me, "You're our guest! Please, sit, enjoy the game."

"Thanks, but I'm not really into football," I say.

The uncle says, "How 'bout that, Markie-boy, you got yourself a girl who likes to cook!"

In the kitchen, the aunt has the ever-present cigarette dangling from her red lips as she checks the turkey. Mark's cousin, Sara, a young mother in her mid-twenties, is peeling potatoes at the table. When they notice me standing in the entryway, Sara smiles, says, "Join the party."

The aunt taps an ash from her cigarette into the sink. She says, in that voice of hers, "Yeah, let's get to know each other. You're the first girl Mark has brought by the house."

I take a seat next to Sara and ask, "What can I do to help?"

The aunt says, "Well, for starters, sweetheart, you can tell us where Mark disappears to."

"Disappears to?"

Sara says, "Mom, come on."

But the aunt is insistent. "He stays out all night and when I worry, he gets mad at me. Is he with you?"

I stammer, "He, ummm, he, that is, uh . . ."

The aunt shakes her head. "I'll take that as a yes. Sweetheart, there are two kinds of girls: the ones boys marry and the ones they have a good time with. You catch my drift?"

Sara gives me a sympathetic look and returns to peeling the potatoes.

When the aunt puts the turkey back in the oven, she says, "Don't let a handsome face make you do things you'll regret. That's all I'm saying, sweetheart."

❖ ❖ ❖

After dinner, Mark drives me all the way back to Morningside Heights in his uncle's old Sunbird. The traffic doesn't seem to bother him all that much. His aunt and uncle, on the other hand . . .

"You see why I have to move out? They're driving me crazy." He imitates his aunt's smoky voice: "Where the hell were you all night? It's Sunday and you're not going to church? What would your parents think? Blah, blah, blah."

"She's just concerned. Anyway, now she's convinced I'm the cheap ho you're sleeping with."

We drive for in silence until Mark says, "Thanks for coming with me. And for lying for me."

I say, imitating his aunt, "It was my pleasure, sweetheart."

He laughs and says, "No, sweetheart, the pleasure was entirely my own."

After Mark drops me off at JJ, I find there's a reward waiting for me: a message from Simon, asking me out for dinner and some live music.

DECEMBER

After the two other *E*s return from their holidays in Michigan and California, I let them know that Simon and I are going out on our THIRD date. They're still a little too thrilled for me, but I don't mind. When I call Mark to tell him, he says he's happy for me. This is the right thing to say, but there's still a tiny part of me that hopes he'll be jealous.

Yes, stupid, I know.

Simon picks me up at JJ — I told him I'd be happy to save him the trip from Long Island to Morningside Heights and meet him downtown, but he insisted on coming up to my room to collect me, like a real gentleman would.

And he's looking quite spiffy, I must say. We're going to share a meal at a funky little Spanish-Thai fusion place in Alphabet City, before heading to the Village to hear a jazz quartet.

I tell Simon, "You look good."

Simon looks at me seriously and says, "You look very nice."

We discuss M theory over a tasty meal and head to the club, which is small and a bit run-down. The tables bear the stains of cigarette burns and spilled drinks and the chairs are a mismatch of dining room chairs, office chairs, and card table chairs. The tiny stage is illuminated by a bright spotlight that makes the quartet of two black and two white men sweat as they perform, and I applaud when Simon does, unsure of how he knows when to clap.

During a break Simon orders us a couple of tap beers that are served in plastic cups (this is not a place that cards). When the waitress sets them down on our tiny cracked table, Simon lifts his toward me and says, "I'd like to propose a toast."

I lift my cup.

He says, "Here's to Molly Swain, imposter jazz fan."

After we take sips from our beer, I shake my head. "Is it that obvious?"

"No, but I'm an expert at imposters. Next time we'll go someplace you want to go. And speaking of places, my parents have finally agreed I should get something closer to Columbia. I can hardly wait. No more commuting from Long Island."

I say, "That's great."

His eyes sparkle for a moment, but then fade. "The only problem is everything's so pricey. Do you know anyone who's looking for a roommate? I don't think I can afford a place of my own."

I say, "Sorry."

Part of me waits for him to ask me if I want to live with him, but, of course, it's waaaay too soon for that. But I would have liked him to ask.

We take another sip of our drinks, and then I blurt out, "This is a date we're on, right?"

Simon seems mildly offended by the question. "It's a date, Molly. You don't think it's a date?"

I hold his hand. I know it was a blunt thing to ask, but after my experience with Mark, I just want to be sure that how I perceive situations is similar to how other people do. I say, "I was hoping it was," as the quartet returns to the stage to open their second set.

The music seems easier to follow, and as I hear the drummer softly beat and the bass player gently pluck, I look at Simon, his intense eyes following the movements of the musicians, as if he's trying to predict their next notes, their next riffs. His profile is completely unlike

Mark's, whose face is more angular and defined. Simon's face seems younger in an odd way, like he's still growing into it.

Simon catches me looking at him and smiles. He whispers, "By the way, my parents are very anxious to meet you. They don't want to wait another *ogenblikje*."

Mark says that if he spends one more minute in Montclair he'll *climb a water tower and thin out the crowd.* He makes the long journey into town so we can grab a cup of coffee at one of the fourteen million Starbucks locations in Manhattan, my treat. He's tired of his painting job and the amount of time he spends with his uncle. He wants a new job, a new place to live, a new life in the city without his aunt and uncle always looking over his shoulder. He's looked at the want ads and the for-rent and roommate-wanted ads, but he's worried he won't find a job that pays enough for rent, food, and the subway.

He stares at his cup of decaf that he's drowned in cream and sugar.

Our new thing is imitating his aunt — isn't it nice that we have a *thing*? — and he says in a deep, hacky voice: "What am I gonna do, sweetheart? I don't wanna go back to Le Sueur and I feel stranded out in Montclair."

I look at his adorable face and sleepy eyes. I say, my voice a phlegmy baritone, "I'm not crazy about the guy, sweetheart, but can't you move in with Jim?"

Mark looks at me sadly. He pretends he's holding a cigarette between his fingers as he says, "Sweetheart, I think all he wants is sex." I laugh, but then Mark drops the aunt voice, saying, "And I think he's been hooking up with other guys."

This gets my attention. "What makes you say that?"

"When I get off work, I want to see him, but he's got all these lame excuses lately. I'm lucky if we get together one or two nights a week. We have sex and he doesn't want me to spend the night. He always has a 'big day tomorrow.'"

I look at my mocha, feeling a bit guilty. Part of me is happy that things are turning sour with Jim. I say, "That doesn't sound promising."

Mark's eyes water, just like that. He says, "I'm in love with him, Moll."

I reach over for his hand. "There's someone much better out there for you. Someone sweet and considerate and intelligent," I tell him.

"But he's got a really hot body."

I sigh, releasing his hand.

Mark says, "Okay, okay. I just hate going over there wondering if this will be the night he tells me it's over. He keeps telling me we don't have very much in common. And I think he's embarrassed by me when we're with his friends. Like I'm some farm boy from the sticks or something."

"You *are* a farm boy from the sticks. That's something to be proud of. Don't let some New York posers get you down. They're a dime a dozen." Then I resume the aunt voice: "Dump him, sweetheart."

He changes the subject. "If only I could actually afford to live here."

That's when it occurs to me. I say, "Maybe you and Simon could go in on a place together."

He frowns. "Simon the boyfriend?"

"Why not, sweetheart?"

I thought it would take some lobbying on my part, but thankfully, Simon thinks finding a place with Mark is a good idea. He only had two questions: 1) How much can Mark afford to pay in rent? and 2) How soon can he move? Simon's picked me up at a Long Island Railroad station and we're in his father's Lexus driving to his house, where his mother has prepared a meal in my honor.

I, Molly Swain, am, at long last, the Girlfriend. Not a straight girl in love with a gay guy, not a beard for a family gathering, but a legitimate Girlfriend.

Simon says, "My parents can't know my roommate's going to be gay," he tells me as he drives through thick traffic.

"He's not *going to be gay*. He is gay."

"You know what I mean."

I consider the buildings as we pass by them and say, "Why not?"

Simon grunts, "I'm an only child. It was tough enough to get my parents to agree to let me move out. I don't want to give them anything else to object to."

I say, "Your parents have always sounded cool."

He mutters, "Try living with them."

I think about Mom in her greasy uniform at Boss Burger with her long gray hair and Dad knocking back a couple of Big Macs behind the wheel of his rig. I wonder what Lily and Jessie and Simon would think of them if they ever met. I wonder why I feel embarrassed at just the prospect of it. With Mark, I don't have to worry about these things.

I finally say, "Mark can play it straight when your parents stop by the apartment. He passed all through high school. He fooled everyone."

When we arrive at Simon's house, we find the driveway lined with luminarias, little candles in white paper bags filled with sand. It gives the home a very elegant look, not that it needed much help. While I'm impressed, Simon embarrassedly refers to the house as a McMansion.

I'm just glad he can't see my home in Le Sueur.

Inside the entryway, which takes up two entire floors with its high ceiling, Simon's father greets me warmly, takes my coat. He has glasses and wears a charcoal sweater that is a nice contrast to his thick gray hair. He's shorter than his son, and this seems to please him. He says, "So nice to meet you, Molly. Simon's told us so much about you."

Simon's mother appears in an apron and pearls, just like in the old TV shows on Nick at Nite. She says, "A pleasure, Molly." To Simon she says, "You didn't tell us how beautiful she is."

Apart from my parents, no one has ever called me beautiful.

We enter the great room where appetizers fill the coffee table: stuffed grape leaves, cheeses of all kinds and descriptions, hot asparagus dip, sliced French bread, and crackers in different shapes, sizes, and textures. From various points along the walls, school portraits of Simon, his parents' only child, stare at us. The early photos feature a happy, smiling boy but as he ages, the smile disappears, replaced by a serious and earnest expression that makes him look much older.

The conversation comes easily: We discuss Columbia, New York, Minnesota, and quantum mechanics, which Simon's parents are familiar with and tolerant of.

Before dinner is served, Simon takes me on a tour of the house, and when we get to his bedroom, it appears to be one giant pile of books, along with a computer and a bed. No posters, no pictures on the walls, no footballs or stuffed animals or religious icons. No clues or insights into Simon at all.

I excuse myself, use his bathroom. I run the water as I open the medicine chest. (Yes, I am an awful person.) But again I'm disappointed, since there's nothing that reveals too much about the guy who filled it. There's just toothpaste, dental floss, shaving cream, razors, deodorant, aspirin, and . . . *hello* . . . a prescription bottle. I look at the door to make sure it's locked, and then back at the bottle.

Zoloft.

Antidepressants, the same kind my aunt Aggie takes. And Simon's name is on the bottle.

I close the cabinet and flush the toilet for good measure.

When I get home later that night, Jessie appears in the doorway and sticks a finger in her mouth, her signal that she's sick of studying and wants a break. Landing with a little grunt on my bed, she says, "Chris stood me up. Again. And now there's nothing to do but study. I'm so bored. What's new?"

I rearrange the books on my desk in order of priority. I think I'm in the minority here, in that I actually read everything assigned. I say, "Simon's getting a place of his own."

This interests Jessie. "Oooh, a little love nest for Molly and the boyfriend. Where is it?"

"He hasn't found an apartment yet, but he's looking. And Mark is going to be his roommate."

Jessie looks at me, an uncertain expression on her face. "Really?"

I frown. "Yeah, really. What's the problem?"

She shrugs. "You sure you want your new boyfriend

and your old love sharing a place? Isn't that kind of . . . I don't know . . . awkward?"

"I am *over* my crush on Mark."

Jessie looks at me, unconvinced. But she doesn't pursue it, just says, "Think about all the note-comparing they can do. You won't have any secrets left."

I sigh. Who needs secrets, anyway?

When I next see Simon in strength training, he's thrilled. He can move out sooner than he thought. He's found a mid-December lease for an apartment in Washington Heights in a largely Dominican neighborhood that's not too far from the subway. He'll finally live away from home, in a small efficiency on the top floor of a four-story walk-up that he will share with Mark (who hasn't even seen it yet, but is just happy to have a place in the city).

On moving day, Lily and I survey the apartment and I wonder why on earth Simon moved out of his parents' beautiful home on Long Island. The apartment's floor is scratched wood with large cracks, the walls a whitish color that was painted over peeling wallpaper. The sink must have been white at one point in history, probably before the Civil War. Now, though, it looks like the rust stains are the only thing holding it together.

And did I mention the cockroaches? Not the live scurrying kind (they are probably waiting for lights-out) but the big, dead, crunchy kind. The landlord must have sprayed before giving Simon the keys. Lily asks, "Did Simon pack a broom and dustpan?"

I look at the floor where the scattered corpses lie in state, awaiting burial. I say, "We can only hope."

Lily says, "I'm having my shoes re-soled after this. Yecch. And why isn't Jessie helping us?"

I sigh. "Chris called at the last minute for an impromptu 'date.'"

Lily shakes her head. "She needs to make herself less available. A *lot* less available."

"It was sweet of Nathan to help out." Nathan is Lily's white boyfriend.

Lily looks grim. "Like I could lose him for even an afternoon. I don't know, sistuh-woman-sistuh, he's just so —"

The sounds of Simon's and Nathan's footsteps stop her in midsentence. They arrive in the apartment with a grunt and drop two heavy boxes of books on the floor, smashing roach corpses to tiny bits in the process. Simon says, "Oy, those weigh a ton."

After we're done hauling the boxes up to Simon's new fourth-floor walk-up, Lily and Nathan head out in search of pizza and pop. Simon just stands in the middle of his little apartment with his hands on his hips, trying to catch his breath. He looks over at me where I sit in a cockroach-free corner, trying to catch my own breath, and says, "Thanks so much for all the help. It was really nice of Lily and Nathan to lend a hand, too."

I half-say/half-gasp, "It's not that you had that much stuff. . . . It's just . . . those four flights of stairs."

He drops to the floor himself now. "No, it was all those books. I don't know why I brought them all. And who knew a futon could weigh so much? I need to get back into my workout routine."

"What are you going to do for a desk and chairs? And plates? And silverware? And bookcases?"

He says, "I've got what I need for now. Besides, my mom loves shopping. I think me getting my own place is a vicarious thrill for her, though she would never admit it. She went straight from her family to marrying my father. She's never had a place of her own."

"Speaking of shopping . . ." I take a small gift-wrapped box out of my bag and hold it up. I say, "It's a house-warming present. If you want it, you're going to have to come over here, because I can't get up."

He crawls over on his hands and knees and I hear the crunch of a roach corpse. Before he takes the box from me, he gives me a little kiss on the lips. He says, "You didn't have to do that. Gimme!"

I bought the antique wooden frame at a flea market in the Village. The black-and-white picture of Simon and me is one Jessie took. In the photo we're smiling, our cheeks touching. While it's a great shot of Simon, I wish it were a better one of me. I look too white, overexposed.

He says thank you and kisses me again, a little longer this time. We both are a bit unsure about kissing. Not that we don't want to; it just seems that neither of us is particularly confident, and it shows. He pulls me up and off the floor, gives me a little hug. Then we start a slow dance to the sounds of the people and traffic outside. I rest my head on his shoulder as we sway back and forth, moving our feet in a slow circle. His body feels strong and he smells of perspiration and Speed Stick. He says, "We should go out dancing for real. You know, someplace that plays the old slow songs."

"Sounds wonderful."

He looks down at me as he stops moving. With his hand, he lifts up my chin before pressing his lips into mine. I think our confidence is growing. And I like the feel of his body next to mine. It makes me feel real. Like I matter to him.

And then there's a loud buzz. From the front door's loudspeaker we hear Lily say, "It's us!"

The lock release doesn't work, so Simon has to walk down the four flights to let them in. I decide to join him and we walk hand in hand down the stairs. I say, "Thanks again for agreeing to share with Mark. I know he's really excited to be moving into the city."

But Simon already seems disappointed in Mark. He says, "He's so excited he couldn't help me move. He will cramp *our* style, if you know what I mean."

I do. For the first time in my life, I do.

At the door, Lily and Nathan hand Simon and me cold bottles of pop and spring water. Lily says, "We got a cheese veggie pizza since we know you two worship Brian Greene, the vegan physicist."

Nathan says, "I so wanted sweet Italian sausage. But it's really long, lean Chinese food I love best."

Lily shakes her head, annoyed. "That's not funny."

Nathan says, "Sorry, babe."

Now Lily looks up at the ceiling and then back at him. "Remember our little talk? I'm not *babe*, I'm not *baby*, and I'm not *honey*. I'm Lily."

"Sorry," Nathan says.

We stand there awkwardly for a moment, Nathan looking at Lily apologetically and Simon and I pretending they just didn't have, as Mom would put it, *a little exchange.* Fortunately, Mark picks that very moment to show up, a single suitcase in hand. He says, "Jeez, I got lost. And this ain't the kind of neighborhood you wanna get lost in."

Simon takes his suitcase, amazed, and says, "Is this all you have?"

Mark says, "I got some more crap in Montclair. It can wait."

I say, "I thought Jim was going to drop you off."

Mark rolls his eyes. "I thought so, too."

Simon's suddenly eager to show Mark their new apartment, so the two of them run up the stairs as Lily and I follow, Nathan a few steps below us, silent and sad. When we enter the apartment, Simon is showing Mark the rusted sink as if it were a sports car. Simon has set his futon in a closet posing as a bedroom, leaving Mark to choose which corner will be his "bedroom."

Simon tells Mark, "We're so lucky to get a mid-month rental!"

It could have been luck. Or it could have been the fact that nobody in their right mind would want to live in a dump like this. But Simon is so excited, it's cute. It's like he's his own little country that just won its war for independence.

I go look out the window as Lily and Nathan set the pizza and drinks out on the kitchen counter. Simon searches through one of his boxes for plates, and Mark joins me as we look out on the crowded street below, alive with cars and pedestrians and music and sirens.

Mark says, "Not exactly Main Street, is it?"

I smile at him. "I do miss Le Sueur. I miss the trees and the sidewalks where you don't have to weave and dodge your way through other people. And I miss the quiet."

He puts an arm around me and it feels good. He says, "I know what you mean. This city can just be . . . I dunno . . . overwhelming. It's always *on*."

I pat his arm. "We'll go back home for Christmas. Have you got your ticket yet?"

He looks at me shyly. "I'm not going back."

I remove his arm, give him a look. "You have to go back! Who am I going to hang out with over break?"

He just says, "Sorry, Moll, but there's no way I'm going back. You'll have to handle it on your own."

Lily shouts, "Come on, Minnesota Twins, the pizza's getting cold!"

With finals coming up, a quadruple date is our last opportunity to have a late night before we sequester ourselves to cram. Mark almost backs out at the last minute — he's working double shifts at his new job, as a cashier at a Duane Reade drugstore near Times Square — but I suspect the real reason he wants to bail is because he and Jim are fighting again.

The Three *E*s have gathered in Jessie's room to apply our finishing touches. I'm wearing a sleeveless blouse and Lily comments on my arms, which actually look strong, thanks to the weight lifting. She says, "Sistuh-woman-sistuh, look at you! You're getting all buff."

I flex my biceps. "I must admit, I do look good. For me."

Lily says, "You look good for anyone."

Jessie is staring at the phone on the desk, when she's not staring at the cell phone in her hand. Unfortunately, she has dyed her hair blond to surprise Chris and hope-fully rekindle his interest. Frankly, it makes her look a bit washed-out and ghostlike. Lily and I tried to talk her out of it, but then her stylist talked her back into it (it cost over one hundred dollars), so here she sits like a traffic light stuck on yellow.

Lily says, "I forget. Do you want him to call or not call?"

Jessie says, "Not call. If he calls, that means he's come up with another lame excuse."

Lily says, "All righty, then."

We finish our makeup without the dreaded phone call, so we head down to the lobby at the appointed time. I find Simon and Nathan standing by the grand piano with Mark and Jim, and Chris, who I wasn't sure actually existed, is standing by the fireplace. After we make our introductions, we head to the subway and catch a train to a little restaurant in Tribeca that specializes in Mexican-French fusion and rosewater martinis.

Chris, who is tall and thin with thick, wavy brown hair, deep-set mocha eyes, and a pointy chin is — I hate to admit it — a charmer. Over appetizers he draws Simon out of his shell and makes Nathan feel like an old friend. He asks Mark and Jim about gay marriage and lets them know that he supports civil unions as they nod politely, maybe feeling a bit uncomfortable being the only same-sex couple at our table.

When the main course arrives, Nathan and Lily tell

us about the latest independent films. Next, Jessie and Chris discuss politics (Chris will be going to law school at NYU and looks forward to running for office after a few years as an assistant district attorney). Jessie's a smart and funny girl with opinions that she doesn't offer in his company. I find this side of her sad and blame Chris, although there's nothing in what he says to indicate he's leading her on or lying to her. He's not dismissive, but he is also not — as my Grammy Hautman used to say — "smitten."

When Chris asks Mark what he's studying, Mark stammers, "I don't go to school."

Chris asks him what he does.

"Working at Duane Reade."

Chris smiles too broadly, says, "That's . . . interesting."

I tell the table, "Mark's a wonderful artist. You should see his drawings."

I'm touched as Simon joins in and defends his new roommate, saying, "Mark's got real talent. You should see his Mad Cow drawings; they should be published as a graphic novel."

Chris says, "Mad Cow?"

Mark mumbles, "It's just a stupid cartoon I do."

I wait for Jim to support Mark, tell him it's not just a stupid cartoon, but he doesn't say anything, just checks his cell phone for messages.

Chris comments that graphic novels are very popular, that there are whole aisles of them at Barnes & Noble and Borders. He encourages Mark to stick with it, start submitting his work.

Now it feels like Simon's and my turn to offer a topic for discussion, and, quite frankly, quantum physics doesn't garner the same interest as films or politics.

Lily tosses us a softball. "So, you two are both bodybuilders?"

I laugh, but Simon's confused. He says, "No."

Lily says, "I mean, you met in weight lifting class."

Simon says, "Oh yeah, strength training. We spot each other. But we're really into physics. I'm going to work in matrix theory."

Chris says, as a little joke, "You mean you're going to dress all in black and travel through phone lines?"

But Simon doesn't get it. "No," he says earnestly before he warms to his favorite topic. "This theory postulates that zero-branes are the fundamental ingredients that come together to create strings as well as higher dimensional branes. If we can prove that matrix theory is accurate, it may mean that strings, branes, maybe even space and time are composed of zero branes. It's very exciting."

The rest of the table looks at us blankly.

I back up for the nonphysicists, who are on their second round of martinis. "Um, strings are tiny filaments. In string theory the fundamental ingredient of nature is not point particles but these filaments."

Mark shoots me a sympathetic look; obviously, his new roommate has been lecturing him on matrix theory.

Simon says, "You know, string theory brings general relativity and quantum mechanics together." He shakes his head as he says, "Finally!" as if everyone else at the table shares his great relief.

Jim says, "I've got to take this," as he leaves with his vibrating cell phone. Mark glares at him as he walks out of the dining room.

After an awkward moment of silence, Chris says to Simon, "General relativity. That's Einstein, right?"

Simon nods. "Right. Relativity is the set of laws that govern very large objects, quantum mechanics the laws of the very small. Think of it as bringing together a space observatory and a microscope. One set of rules for what we see in outer space, another for inner space. And the only way these laws work together is through string theory."

"Sounds interesting," Chris says in the same exact tone my father uses when I try to explain it to him.

I smile, say, "We're really enjoying strength training." I flex my biceps.

Chris says, "Wow, impressive."

But Simon doesn't take the hint. He says, "Don't you see? There are two primary schools in physics. One school is for the very large scale, things like stars and galaxies. And the other school is for atoms and molecules and subatomic particles like electrons and quarks. But the laws of one were useless in the other and vice versa. And how can that be? They can't both be right. It was the elephant in the living room of physics! And conflicting laws have been around forever in physics. I mean, just go back to Newton's laws of motion and Maxwell's laws of electromagnetism. Incompatible!"

Chris says, "Sounds just like what I expect law school to be. Contradictory laws. So Molly, what do you think of New York? Jessie tells me you're from Minnesota."

"Le Sueur, home of the Jolly Green Giant!" Jessie offers.

Mark snaps out of his funk, says, "I'm from Le Sueur, too. Moll and I —"

But Simon interrupts him. "Einstein was able to

make motion and electromagnetism compatible through general relativity. And now the challenge is the incompatibility of quantum and relativity. If matrix theory is right, and I believe it is, well, imagine the possibilities for understanding the nature of existence."

Chris rubs his eyes, calls over the waiter, points to our table, and says, "Another round, please."

Mark looks at me, trying not to laugh. I'm not proud of what I'm thinking: 1) that Simon is a nerd with no social skills, and 2) that being his girlfriend diminishes me in the eyes of my friends. When it's just Simon and me, I don't feel this way. But in a group . . .

To take the spotlight off of Simon and their lowering opinion of him, I say, "I'm already freaking out about finals."

Mark says, "You'll ace them, Moll." He tells the group, "Molly's the reason I got an A in chemistry."

Simon says, "You were a tutor in high school?"

Mark says, "Nah, she let me copy her answers."

Simon looks at me closer now, slightly alarmed. "Why did you do that?"

Lily and Jessie exchange looks. Mark still doesn't know that I helped him because I was in love with him. So I say, "Just being a friend."

Simon looks at Mark and then back at me. He says, "Oh."

Jessie says, "I let my friends cheat off of all my tests in high school."

To be helpful, Lily adds, "I still do!"

After settling the bill, Nathan, Mark, and Simon escort Lily and me back to JJ while Jessie leaves with Chris to go to his place for some "coffee." Simon has to go back to the apartment to study, and while Nathan wants to hang out with us, Lily tells him she has to study, too.

When it's just Lily, Mark, and me in her room, she puts on the Last Refuge of the Damned to make us some coffee. She and Mark are buzzed from the martinis but I'm stone-cold sober since I couldn't even finish one.

Lily says, "Simon's a nice guy, but come on. Nearly an hour on the mathematical difficulties to be resolved if matrix theory is to work? I could feel my eyes glazing over."

I say, "Well, Simon can talk about it all night long. I just wish it hadn't been tonight."

"You can say *that* again."

And while I was mortified when Simon kept going on and on about matrix theory, I feel protective of him now. "He's a perfectly nice guy."

Lily says, "I didn't say he wasn't."

I say, "He just makes your eyes glaze over."

Lily says, "You're being defensive."

I say, "No I'm not."

But Mark has to agree with Lily. "Try living with him. He won't shut up about it. It's like he's trying to convert me to some cult."

I look at him sitting on Lily's desk, all good looks and sleepy eyes, and I say, "At least *my* boyfriend doesn't just get up and walk out on a dinner." And without paying his share of the tab.

Now Mark looks hurt and I feel like a jerk. I say, "Sorry, I didn't mean that."

Mark tries to smile and says, "It's okay. You're right; he was an ass."

Lily looks at the two of us and says, "Come on. There's a party down the hall; let's go crash it."

With the holidays close at hand, Mom and Dad are calling more often, excited about seeing their Sweet Pea again after so many months apart. I'm excited to see them — and even Russ — but they don't get why I have to end our conversations early since they've never had a finals week themselves. The only class I feel truly confident about is strength training.

Simon and I mostly just e-mail each other with updates.

> Si-Man
>
> If I never read another "important" literary book in my life I will die a happy, happy woman. The problem with Virginia Woolf is that she didn't walk into the river soon enough.
>
> Say hi to Mark for me and give yourself a big old wet one on those O-brane lips of yours.
>
> Me

And his reply:

> Hey Molly
>
> My brains are awash in quantum fluctuations thanks to the uncertainty principle, in my case the uncertainty that I can keep all these pieces of

useless information in my head until finals are over. Mark's so funny. He says I should just copy the answers off your tests like he did. If only it were that easy/possible.

A multiverse of luck to you.

Simon

After I make it back to my room with a large black coffee (no cream or sugar), there's another e-mail waiting for me from Simon.

It finally happened. There are no vacant cells left in my brain in which to store knowledge. Whenever I try to cram a fact in one side something pops out the other. I was a 4.0 student in high school but I think I'm going to get my first Bs this semester. I wish we had more time.

P.S. Mom wants to have you over on Friday for dinner before you leave for break. She really likes you.

I smile, so grateful that Simon's mom likes me.

And then for a moment I wonder if I like Simon. I frown.

Of course I like Simon. He's my boyfriend. We have so much in common.

Or maybe I just want a boyfriend, and anyone will do.

Or maybe I'm still in love with Mark.

Ridiculous. I just need to pull a *My Fair Lady* with Simon so he can hold a conversation that doesn't begin and end with M theory. And I just love having Mark as a friend.

The coffee tastes like pure acid and I can't finish it. I look at my notes from Lit Hum and wish I could motivate myself to show at least one brane of interest in them. Fortunately, the phone rings and I have a legitimate diversion.

"Is Mark there?"

Oh good, it's Jim.

I say, "No."

"Do you have his number?"

I lie. "No."

"He won't give me his new number. Tell him I'm sick of waiting around for him to call me."

I flip the bird at the phone as I ask, "Any other sweet nothings you want me to pass on?"

"Is he seeing somebody else?"

"I hope so. You are."

I hear Jim blow some frustrated air out of his lungs. "He just came on too strong. You don't come out of the closet and walk directly down the aisle."

"If you want to talk to Mark, wait for *him* to call *you*."

Jim snaps, "Just tell him to call me," and then the line goes dead.

Mark can do so much better.

Somehow, the Three *E*s survive finals week. Our grades won't be posted right away, so there's nothing to do but obsess and do some Christmas shopping. In Central Park, Jessie treats us to a carriage ride, complete with hot chocolate and a horse wearing a Santa hat with a jingle bell on the end. It's been a very good semester, and I feel grateful for my friends and for Simon and for the entire city of New York, which has opened up my eyes to things beyond string theory and loneliness.

As our carriage makes its way over a small bridge I wonder how I ever got out of high school alive. On a good day I'd be left alone and not the butt of some joke or nasty crack. A bad day was a Donna Piambino day. I must have been a stronger person than I gave myself credit for. I wrap my arms around Lily and Jessie, and we sing *Christmas is coming, the goose is getting fat. Now why would the gander do a thing like that?*

After we're done, I say good-bye to Lily and Jessie. I still have an errand left on my Christmas list.

I'm at Mark's Duane Reade, not far from Times Square. I chat as he rings up customers, tourists buying alarm clocks and middle-aged women buying anti-wrinkle creams. He's glad to see me, but nervous that he'll get in trouble for socializing during his shift.

A man with a thick German accent asks him, "Plugs for de ears, please."

Mark points to an aisle, adding, "Halfway down and on the rack to your left."

I say, "Well, this must beat the Le Sueur Super America." Mark worked there the summer between our junior and senior years.

He says, "Sometimes I miss it. This place is always busy. And in Le Sueur, all you had to know was English and a little Spanish to help the customers. Here anything goes: Russian, French, German, Japanese, Hebrew,

Chinese, Italian. Half the time I don't even recognize the language."

I offer: "I can teach you how to say *One moment, please* in Dutch."

He looks at me with his exceedingly handsome face. I ask him, "What's Simon saying about me these days? Does he pine away the hours whilst we're apart?"

Mark frowns. *"Whilst?"*

I say, "It's like *when.*"

He says, "Not really. You know Simon. It's all about M theory."

I'm disappointed, but I guess that's why Simon is Simon.

Mark says, "You remember my cousin Sara from Thanksgiving?"

"Of course I remember, sweetheart."

"I told her that I'm gay, sweetheart."

I'm thrilled. Finally, he has a family member he can be honest with. I say, "That's great!"

He says, "Well, she's a Unitarian; I thought if anyone could handle it, she could."

"What are you going to do for Christmas?"

He says as he watches for potential shoplifters, "Spend it with Sara and her family. Dinner with my aunt and uncle."

I look at his sleepy eyes and say, "You know, you really should come back to Le Sueur with me. If money's an issue, I can lend you the airfare. I've been really good about my budget this fall." Okay, that last part is a complete lie, but at least I'm not broke. Well, not *completely* broke, anyway.

He says, "I dunno . . ."

"Please? *Please, please, please, please?* We'll have a lot of fun — we can hang out at the cemetery and talk and just chill out. Come on, you *have* to come back with me. Who am I going to talk to?"

He looks at me, puzzled. "You can hang with your family."

I sigh. "But they won't get it."

"Get what?"

I hesitate before I say, "What my life is like now."

He smiles at me, and then he says, "Thanks, Moll. You're the only one who gets what my life is like now, too. Tell you what — once you get back home to NYC, we'll have a few brews and you can give me all the news from Le Sueur."

I pout. "I guess."

"How 'bout we go out dancing when you get back. You can meet some of my new friends."

"What new friends?"

He says, "You know, dudes to go out dancing with and shit."

"Good. Maybe one of them will replace Jim."

"I do have my eye on someone new."

"Fork over the details."

"I don't want to jinx it. Hey, I have your Christmas gift. I was gonna wrap it and bring it 'round JJ." From under the counter he pulls out a little bag. "For you."

I'm about to open it when he says, "Hey, wait till Christmas morning!"

I pull a small wrapped box from my purse and present it to him. I say, "I was hoping to give this to you on Christmas day, but since you aren't coming back to Le Sueur with me . . . well, here. Merry Christmas."

He takes it from me, saying, "Hey, thanks, Moll."

Another customer interrupts us. This one is buying cigarettes and vitamins. After Mark rings her up, I tell him, "Well, go on, open it."

He rips off the wrapping paper and bow and opens the box, which contains a silver ring, just a simple band. He looks at me, smiling and confused. I tell him, "It's a friendship ring. To commemorate everything that's happened."

He seems touched. He says, "Thanks, Moll." He tries

to slip it on his right hand, but it doesn't quite fit his ring finger.

I frown. "I was worried about that. We'll have to get it resized."

Now he slides it on his pinky finger and says, "No, don't worry. It's perfect."

All at once, what looks like a swarm of customers descends upon Mark. I smile and wave good-bye. Once I'm out the doors I open the bag. He's filled it with my favorite lipstick and eye shadow, along with the shampoo and toothpaste I like.

I know he probably didn't pay for it, but it's a sweet gesture.

Simon's mother is serving appetizers as we sit in the great room, where studio portraits of Simon stare at us from the white walls. After I tell her about my day with the girls, she says, "Shopping in Manhattan. Is there anything more fun than that? I'm so glad you got out and enjoyed yourself. There's more to life than studying, after all."

Simon says, "How come there's more to *her* life than studying, but not more to *mine?*"

She says, "Please, you put more pressure on yourself to be a straight-A student than your father and I ever have. And on Molly's behalf, let me say she adds the 'more' to your life. Honestly, you're so thoughtless at times I can't believe you're mine."

Dinner is served in the dining room, which has been outfitted with good china and crystal glasses. At one end sits Simon's mother; at the other, Simon's father, who had to be convinced to join us, saying he "didn't want to spoil the young people's good time." I sit across from Simon as I wonder what Mark would think of this house, so different from the little home he shared with his parents on their farm.

Simon's father says to me, "You're leaving us tomorrow for an entire month! What'll we do without you, Molly?"

I say, "Heave a sigh of relief?"

He says, "Aw, Molly, don't even kid. I'll be crying my eyes out the moment your plane leaves the ground. And what about my poor boy? I bet you two kids will be on the phone to each other every single day."

Simon says, "Dad."

Simon's father asks me, "What's the point of having a son if you can't embarrass him in front of his girl?" To me he says, "What will you do for an entire month in Le Sewer?"

"Le Sueur. Spend time with my family, finally see some movies that my friend Lily doesn't approve of, maybe go to the Cities and do some Christmas shopping."

Simon's mother says, "I've never been to the Twin Cities. But I did love *The Mary Tyler Moore Show* when I was a girl. What was that song, again . . . ?"

Simon's father sings, "Love is all around, no need to something, you can never tell, why don't you something."

Simon's mother laughs but her son cringes.

The meal passes quickly and comfortably, at least for Simon's parents and me. Simon himself looks like he keeps waiting for something to go wrong and when nothing does, he seems neither relieved nor disappointed.

In the kitchen, I help his mother load the dishwasher. She asks me if I've ever been to temple and I tell her honestly, no, I never have. She says maybe I could join them sometime before she tells me that her son once had this odd idea in his head that he could only date Jewish girls in high school. "I don't know where he came up with that," she says as she hands me some plates. "So he didn't go to his senior prom as his way of rebelling against us. And we didn't even have a clue he was rebelling!" She laughs now and shakes her head. "I just thought he couldn't get a date!" She looks like she almost admires her son's stubbornness. She says, "I may have said at some point in my life that it would be nice if he went with a Jewish girl, but I never put any restrictions on him."

I say, "I never dated in high school, either, and my parents never put any restrictions on me." Then I think about Mark, and all the restrictions that everyone put on him, without even realizing we were doing it.

Simon's mother says, "A beautiful young woman like you never dated? I find that hard to believe. Probably like Simon, always with your head in a book. He told me about your scholarship. Very impressive."

I blush.

She says in a conspiratorial whisper, "I know it might not look it, but he's much happier these days, my son. I give you all the credit."

"I'm much happier these days, too."

She winks at me. "Good. And if he gets all morose again or starts talking about matrix theory until you can't take it one more minute, you have my permission to give him a little kick in the pants."

With the dishwasher humming, Simon's parents excuse themselves, leaving us alone in the great room. Simon puts on some classical music and lights a candle. Then he sits next to me on the couch and puts an arm around me. He says, "Thanks for coming out tonight."

I lean my head back, let it rest on his arm as it tilts toward his neck, which has a five-o'clock shadow. I say, "I had a nice time."

He leans into me now, presses his lips against mine.

It feels amazing.

Then we're seriously making out.

And I think: I could go all the way with this guy.

I think I might be in love. I love how this feels. I think it could go further.

Tentatively, I guide his hand under my skirt.

Simon pulls away. He looks at me, blurry-eyed, and says, "Are you sure?"

"I think I am. Do you think we should go to your room?"

He says, "I want you to be sure you're sure."

I hear myself say, "I am."

"I don't think you are."

I pull his face to mine and we kiss, but then Simon pulls away with a gasp.

I open my eyes, asking, "What's —"

And then I see him: Simon's father in a bathrobe, looking as mortified as I feel. He stammers, "I just . . . came down . . . for . . . my midnight snack. . . ."

I look at my feet.

I hear his father tiptoe to the kitchen, open the refrigerator.

I say, ashamed, "I should go home."

Simon doesn't say a word, and as we sit in our embarrassed silence I see Simon's father move like a cat burglar from the kitchen, across the great room, and toward the stairs. Without looking at us he says, "Excuse me again. Very sorry. Good night."

Simon says, "I'll take you home."

I was afraid Simon's parents would think I was a hoochie mama, but instead they made Simon promise that I would not take the M60 bus to LaGuardia for my flight home, even though it's the cheapest option. They think it's too dangerous. When I first arrived in this city I would have agreed with them, but now, after getting acclimated, and having mastered the art of being present on the subway or the bus without engaging any of the other passengers, I have to disagree with them. I think once the unfamiliar becomes familiar, you can begin to find beauty in it.

For example: One day when I was taking the subway to Times Square, a day-care class entered my train at Lincoln Center. The boys and girls were all different colors, each one holding on to a buddy with one hand and a long cord that connected them all with the other as the adults herded them on board. They were loud and friendly and had no idea that so many out-of-towners are afraid to take the subway, that they don't like having to look straight up when they're out on the street in order to see a piece of sky, that they hate the congestion and noise and crowds. To those little kids on my subway train, it was all normal and familiar and fun. And their fellow passengers, no matter their color or age or language, smiled at the kids.

I guess that's why I wouldn't have minded taking the bus to LaGuardia. Yes, this city has more than its fair share of maniacs and posers, but underneath the façade is a big heart, breaking and healing every single moment. It just seems vibrant with possibilities.

This is what I'm thinking when Simon honks his horn outside of JJ's lobby. It will probably take him almost as long to go from Washington Heights to Morningside Heights to Queens and then back home as it will for me to fly from New York to Minneapolis.

He pops the trunk and Mark appears from out of the passenger door. I say, "Hey, I didn't expect to see you here."

He waves to me with his ringed finger and says, "Simon and I are gonna work out. I need to get buff. You should see what the dudes in the clubs look like." Mark helps me load my bags.

I say, "Are you *sure* you don't want to head back with me?"

Mark grimaces and says, *"Positive."*

I say, defeated, "Just asking," and kiss him on the cheek.

In the car, Simon is jumpy. He admits that he doesn't like to drive in the city, and his cautious style makes the cabbies insane. When we're in Queens, he's calmed down . . . but just a little. Every now and again the things he says reminds me that he's his parents' son. He asks me, "You have your ticket?"

I run a hand through his hair. "Of course."

He risks a glance at me as he says, "Just open your purse and double-check."

I sigh, open the purse, hold up the ticket where he can see it.

"And your parents have your arrival time and gate number."

"Yes."

When we pull up to my terminal Mark unloads while Simon and I hold each other, tentatively at first, but then, well, we get over ourselves and kind of make out, just like in the movies. When we're done, Mark is looking at us with a perplexed expression on his face, which I find endearing. I say, "Sorry about the public display of affection. I know it's a form of what Lily calls *heterosexual privilege*."

Mark rolls his eyes before he gives me a hug and whispers in my ear, "Have a safe flight, Molly."

I say, "Your lips to God's ears, sweetheart."

He holds me at arm's length and says, "Have a merry Christmas. And if you see my folks . . ."

"I'll tell them you're fine. Nothing else."

"Cool."

Simon gives me one last hug and a kiss on my cheek. He says, "Have a safe trip. And call when you get home, so my parents don't worry themselves to death."

"I'll use the calling card your mom gave me. Well, boys, this is it. See ya next year."

They stand by the car as I make it through the crowded terminal doors. When I turn around to give them one last wave, they've already gone.

When the plane makes its final approach to the Minneapolis-St. Paul International Airport, passengers look out the windows expecting plains of white snow, only to find an ugly brown landscape. Dad told me that this year has set yet another record for high temperatures and they're not counting on a white Christmas, which I find bitterly disappointing. As a Minnesota gal, a white Christmas is something you depend on.

Once the pilot turns off the seat belt sign, people in the aisle seats pop up like prairie dogs from their holes. They scramble to open overhead bins and grab their carry-ons. Stuffed to overflowing in my backpack, purse, and carry-on bag are the gifts I brought back from New York. Now that we're here, on Minnesota soil, I miss my family more than I ever thought I would. The flight attendants smile and nod as I step on the ramp.

I sprint down the corridor and there, on the other side of the security checkpoint, just where I left them, are Mom, Dad, and Russ. As a joke, Russ is holding a small sign like the chauffeurs have, with the name MS. MOLLY-POP printed on it in neat block letters.

I think this is the first group hug every member of my family has ever voluntarily participated in. Dad's weepy as he says, "Oh, we missed you so much, Sweet Pea!" As our embrace comes to an end, Russ smacks me lightly on the back of the head just to remind me things haven't changed *too* much.

Mom gasps, "Look at your hair! And your makeup!"

Russ adds, "And you've lost weight."

I look at Dad, and I think my new appearance might be a little too much for him. He's used to the heavy Molly with her hair in a ponytail. The new pudgy-but-not-heavy Molly just needs to lose another ten pounds and spends way too much time on her hair and makeup. Still, compared to a lot of other girls at JJ,

I'm a boy. Dad says, "You look beautiful. But then, you always have."

"When was that?" Russ asks, and Mom smacks him on the back of the head.

The drive back to Le Sueur makes me nostalgic. (Is it too early to be nostalgic? I've only been gone four months, but it seems like a lifetime.) In the back-seat of the Skylark, I whisper to Russ, "Stick out your tongue." And there it is: the tongue stud Mom had told me about, still in place in spite of Dad's threats to "rip it out of his mouth." After we take our exit, we go down Main Street, past the Aqua Shine, the Holiday Station, the Le Sueur Motel, the United Farmers Cooperative grain towers, and the tiny home that was the birthplace of the Mayo brothers, founders of the Mayo Clinic in Rochester. The town is outfitted for the holidays, and plastic Santa Clauses and nativity scenes decorate many of the yards that are drought brown from lack of snow. The streets are virtually empty.

When we pull up to our house, I discover that Dad has bought a huge inflatable snowman for the yard. The snowman sways back and forth as an air pump keeps him full. Dad sees me staring and says, "Wait, wait, stay right there! You haven't seen the best part yet!" He runs into the house and suddenly the snowman is illuminated. From the front door, Dad shouts, "Impressive, isn't he? I figure if we can't make a snowman, we might as well buy one."

I shift my gaze from the snowman to my father, who's beaming. I say, "Looks great."

Inside, Mom is heating up some whole milk for hot chocolate, and Dad gives me some souvenirs from his latest trips: a can of birch beer from Pennsylvania, a refrigerator magnet in the shape of Indiana, a little stuffed bear wearing a tiny Toledo sweatshirt. Russ shows me his new games, including one that he thinks I'd enjoy, since it's set in New York. But I take a pass. I'm anxious to get to my room, hide my gifts, and get settled for the long break in Le Sueur.

Mom's made a special dinner of baked chicken with all the trimmings in honor of my homecoming. The table is set with a tablecloth and the good dishes, and two candles glow at the center of the table. The music is a compilation of Christmas classics from the fifties and sixties, and I smile as I hear Al Martino sing Dad's favorite, "You're All I Want for Christmas," already an oldie when he was a kid.

Although we rarely say grace, Mom has us fold our hands in prayer as she says, "Bless us, O Lord, for these thy gifts, which we are about to receive, from thy bounty, through Christ the Lord." Usually, she just finishes with an amen, but tonight she adds, "And thank you, Lord, for bringing our Molly home safe and sound, and for looking after her this fall in New York. Amen."

"Amen," the rest of us say.

"Everything looks wonderful, Mom. You shouldn't have gone to all the trouble."

Mom waves her hand at me. "It's no trouble. You'll understand when you're a mother someday. I've been waiting for you to come home since the day you left."

Dad plops about five pounds of mashed potatoes on his plate, saying, "Some Dahl woman called wondering when you'd get home."

I freeze. "Mark's mom?"

He nods. "Wants to stop by and see you while you're back."

I just nod and help myself to the glazed carrots. I know what's coming next.

Mom says, "Well, how about that, Molly? Mark's mother wants to see you."

I say softly, "How about it. . . ."

Fortunately, Russ interrupts with, "Molly-Pop, you want to go to the Mall of America tomorrow? I'm not done with my Christmas shopping. I'll treat for lunch."

I take it as a good sign that Russ is willing to be seen with me in public, even if it means driving nearly an hour to go to the Mall of America.

I say, "Sure," and then tell Russ, "You're getting an early start on your shopping. For you, I mean."

Russ looks at Dad, confused. Dad says, "Sweet Pea, your old man's gonna be on the road this Christmas. We're going to celebrate a few days early."

"What?"

"You know I make a lot more during the holidays."

For a moment I'm six years old again, pouting in the corner. "You're always gone at Christmas. And New Year's. And every day in between."

We eat in silence for a few moments.

Dad says, "The chicken's delicious."

Mom says, "Thanks."

And I wonder where the scholar from New York has disappeared to.

It's a little surreal to be Christmas shopping in Manhattan one day and in the Mall of America the next. We park in a ramp the size of Le Sueur and stash our coats in the trunk, since the weather is unseasonably warm. (Unseasonable is the new seasonal.) Inside, there are shoppers everywhere, and while some people stride along irritably or happily, others stagger by, their eyes glazed over, overwhelmed by the sheer amount of choices. The tourists from Japan and Saudi Arabia are easy to spot, and I wonder what they must think about the U.S. if this is their only experience in America. The mall has level upon level packed with major retailers and specialty shops; there's even an entire store dedicated exclusively to kitchen magnets.

Russ leads us to a CD store where he looks for appropriate music for Mom and Dad. He wants a late-eighties hits compilation, something that will remind our parents of the good old days. I wonder what they would have studied if they had been able to go to college. I try to imagine Mom writing poetry or Dad taking a criminal justice course (since he loves *Law & Order* so much).

Russ, who is currently a straight-C student, is annoyed. "All these compilations are so lame."

I frown at the display units. "Just get them stuff on CD that they already have on tape."

Russ says, "How about *Born in the USA?*"

"That would work —"

And then, from the corner of my eye, I see her.

Donna Piambino.

The enemy.

Russ looks at me, concerned. "Molly?"

She carries an obscene number of shopping bags from stores that sell the kind of crap you would expect a total and complete bitch in need of maximum slappage to buy. She looks up from her bags and sees me staring at her. She smiles, confused.

Maybe it's my hair, maybe it's the pounds I've dropped, or maybe it's because I now make myself up every day, but she doesn't recognize me immediately. I watch her as she scans her memory and then the lightbulb goes off over her head and she remembers. If only that lightbulb would pop and the falling shards blind her.

She walks over tentatively, saying, "Molly Swain? I wasn't sure that was you. Boy, do you look different."

"You look exactly the same," I tell her. Actually, she doesn't; her face looks fat to me.

"Thanks," she says, like it was a compliment. "Great hair. And you've dropped some pounds. You look amazing."

Russ stares at us, confused. Donna is giving off a friendly vibe, but I'm a long-range ballistic missile just given the go code.

I say, "Shopping?"

Donna shrugs, says, "Yeah, I got a ton of stuff left to buy, but I couldn't resist getting myself a few gifts, too."

"I'm just tagging along with my brother. I did all my shopping in Manhattan."

"Oh," she says.

"All the flagship stores are on Park Avenue. But what I really love is all the little out-of-the-way shops in Soho and the East Village. Some great restaurants there, too. My boyfriend and I love to eat out." I look around deliberately. "We don't have anything like the Mall of America in New York." Then I add: "Thank God."

Donna finally clues in. She says, "I've wanted to drop you a line or send you a card or something. You know, to apologize."

Russ says, "I'll be at Old Navy," and walks away at a brisk pace.

I fold my arms across my chest, feel my face begin to blaze. "A card?" I can't help myself, so I add, "You made my life a living hell for four years and you were going to send me *a card*?"

She looks at me with what I could swear — if I didn't know her better — is sincerity. "I know. Pretty lame, huh? I guess my hormones are making me sappy. I feel bad about the things I did."

I look at her, "Your hormones?"

"I'm pregnant. Baby's due in March."

I look at her more carefully now, but with her coat on and all the shopping bags, it's impossible to tell she's six months along. "Oh."

She says, "I know, isn't it exciting? Dave and me are going to get married in June. Our little angel will be at her mommy and daddy's wedding." Dave, aka *Thirsty Dave*, was her lab partner, a football player with a shaved head who partied much too hard and liked to shoot deer, ducks, pheasants, raccoons, moose, bears, squirrels, cats — basically, anything with a pulse. I can only imagine that his daughter will pop out of Donna with an orange hunting jacket already on, and an empty six-pack tied to the umbilical cord.

"Are you going to college?" I ask her.

"That'll have to wait."

"What's Dave doing?"

"He's at Cambria, working production."

Cambria makes quartz surfaces — countertops. In days gone by, Thirsty Dave might have worked for Green Giant, but with all the mergers and acquisitions, the only jobs they still have in Le Sueur are R&D, which I worked this past summer. Green Giant left — if you'll pardon the expression — some big shoes to fill in terms of decent jobs, and so far, nobody has filled them. Cambria, though, is a good place to end up, I suppose. I ask Donna, "And what are you doing?"

She says, "Just doing temp work for the time being."

Eighteen years old, six months pregnant by Thirsty Dave, and working temp.

In a small voice she asks, "How are you doing? I mean it, you just look . . . great."

"New York is amazing. The art, the culture, the clubs. And I'm loving college. I'm considering a semester abroad. Paris, London, who knows?" Yes, I could add more or make up something else to further emphasize the difference between us, but I let the moment pass. I still think she deserves maximum slappage, but a future with Thirsty Dave is slappage to the tenth power.

Donna looks around. If she's hoping for forgiveness, she's asking too much. She says, "Well, good to see you. Have a merry Christmas."

"You, too."

And then she heads out, alone, balancing the shopping bags filled with things she probably can't afford.

Russ is sixteen and he's driving us home. At first I thought it was a good idea — he needs more highway experience, particularly in the busy lanes of suburban America — but sitting in the passenger seat, my hands balled into fists, my breathing shallow, I realize much too late that this was one of my stupider ideas. I gasp, "Russ, indicate when you're going to change lanes."

An SUV he just swerved in front of honks its horn. Russ looks in the rearview and flips the driver the bird. He says, "Chillax, Molly-Pop, I know what I'm doing."

Right. And Mark can't get enough of my sexy female body. "Why don't you take the next exit and I'll drive us home?"

I expect him to ignore me, but he does as I ask. At a gas station we trade places, and as I put the car in gear, he says, "Sorry, didn't mean to freak you out."

I glance at him. "You didn't freak me out." After that lie, I change the subject. "How're things at school?"

"Boring," he tells me.

"How are things at home?"

"Boring," he says. "Mom works and Dad's on the road all the time."

"So you're drinking and getting high. That's what Mom tells me."

He doesn't say anything.

I follow a Grand Cherokee with a yellow Support Our Troops ribbon magnet on it. I say, "Sorry things are so dull for you. But lay off the booze and the pot."

Russ looks out his window, says, "It's so cool that you're in New York and everything. I tell everybody that you live in Manhattan and go to all the cool clubs."

I smile and pass the Grand Cherokee. "Really? So I'm cool now, huh?"

He looks at me seriously, as if he were a doctor making a diagnosis. "Yeah, I'd say so. Most definitely. I mean, New York and shit, that's so cool. Mom and Dad won't even let me go to the Cities with my friends unless a parent comes with. That's so lame."

"Why do you want to go to the Cities?"

"Dude-ette, the under-21 nights at the clubs are so cool. They play really cool music and the crowd's so cool, you know, with the Cities kids and everything. And the females are sooo hot and they come in all colors. I made out with a Goth chick."

"Don't tell me you had that thing in your tongue."

"Uh, Molly-Pop, her tongue was pierced, too. Don't knock it unless you've tried it and tried it and tried it."

When we get home I read Simon's latest e-mail:

Subject: Christianity

My mom dragged me to the mall with her to buy Christmas gifts for her friends. The place was wall-to-wall with desperate gentiles hunting for the perfect gift. Who needs that kind of pressure? Remind me, what is this holiday all about again?

S.

I e-mail him back.

Subject: RE: Christianity

As all good Christians know, we must celebrate the birth of our savior by spending all our money and baking our own weight in Christmas cookies for the people we like and fruitcakes for the ones we don't. We further honor our Lord by running each other over in parking lots with our cars and in stores with our shopping carts.

What can I say, virgin births make people do crazy things. My advice to our Hebrew friends? When your messiah does arrive, make sure it's the old-fashioned way.

Missing you,

M

There are also e-mails from Lily and Jessie, which make me happy. Lily is distressed because Nathan is calling way too much, while Jessie is thrilled because Chris missed her enough to have phone sex. I've tried to get hold of Mark to give him all the latest from Le Sueur, but he never picks up — working double holiday shifts, no doubt.

On Christmas Day itself, Dad is somewhere between Minnesota and Maryland. Mom's wearing the retro sweater I got her at a consignment shop in the East Village, and Russ has on a club shirt I got him in Soho. Since we had turkey with all the trimmings a few days ago for our "early" Christmas, Mom surprises us by making a pizza with organic sausage and feta cheese. It's part of her campaign to convince me that New York isn't the *be-all, end-all.* I guess I've been a bit annoying with all my comments about New York and how Manhattan compares to Le Sueur.

For example, I made fun of the midnight mass last night and said out loud that I wished I were at St. Patrick's Cathedral, which is huge and beautiful and even though I'm not convinced there is a God, if I were him (or her), I would prefer to watch over my flock in a setting like St. Patrick's rather than St. Anne's. Mom had whispered to me, in an angry voice, "Molly, you're not in New York at the moment, and I'm so sorry that you have to put up with us rubes out here in the back forty." I apologized, but in reality I do miss New York. I mean, once you've seen one Wal-Mart, you've seen them all.

Anyway, that is what I'm thinking about when the doorbell rings, interrupting the DVD we're watching, *It's a Wonderful Life.* I tell Mom and Russ to stay where they are, with their plates balanced on their laps, and answer the door.

There, on the front porch, is Mark's mother, a stream of cigarette smoke pouring out of her pursed lips. I've only met her once, briefly, during commencement, but she made an impression. Her dark roots are clearly visible. Her free hand is in the pocket of a down coat, not that it's all that cold out.

She looks at me suspiciously and says, "Merry Christmas, Molly. You're looking well."

I just stare at her for a moment, then remember to say, "Thanks. Merry Christmas."

"May I come in?"

"Do you mind putting that out?" I ask, pointing to her cigarette. She drops it on the step, stamps it out with a boot.

When Mom sees Mrs. Dahl enter the sitting room, she pauses the DVD. To Russ, she says, "Give me a hand in the kitchen, why don't you?"

"We just sat down," Russ protests.

Mom says, "Now," and they disappear.

I motion toward the couch, my way of offering Mrs. Dahl a seat. She sits with a small grunt. Before I can say a word, she tells me, "I'm sorry to just drop by unannounced on Christmas. I kept hoping Mark would give me a call, but we've had no word from him since he moved out of my sister's place. She has no idea where to find him. But I'm hoping you do. She told me you two were friends. She actually told me you were his girlfriend, that he brought you 'round for

Thanksgiving dinner. But you're not really his girlfriend, are you?"

I cross my arms and legs. Why can't I be his girlfriend? Because he's too good-looking to go with someone like me? I should tell her I'm pregnant.

She looks up at the ceiling, sighing. "I just don't know how to get through to him. It's not normal, the way he's dropped his father and me from his life. It's like we did something wrong, and I have no idea what it was."

She tilts her head, looks at nothing in particular. "Would you give me his phone number and address, please?"

"I, umm . . . I don't have them on me. I'll ask him to call you when I get back to New York, if that's okay."

She rubs her eyes, frustrated. "I didn't come here to argue with you. I want to know where Mark is. I'm worried sick about him. Please, if you know where Mark is, you have to tell me."

I hear myself say, "He's in New York. He's happy. You don't have to worry about him."

Then she just says it. "He's homosexual, isn't he?"

Oh.

Oh.

She sighs. "So he is."

I don't say anything.

"Is he with someone? Someone like . . . him?"

"I don't think he's seeing anyone right now."

She stands to leave. As she heads slowly toward the door, she turns back to me and says, "Okay. Just ask him to call me. *Please.* If he's worried about what we think of his . . . personal life, tell him not to bother. I just want to hear his voice and know he's okay."

Once Mrs. Dahl is out the door, Mom appears in the sitting room, her arms folded across her chest. "What did you tell her?"

"I told her Mark's in New York and that he's happy and that she shouldn't worry about him."

"Anything else?"

"She already knows the rest."

"Of course she does. Mothers aren't as stupid as their children imagine." Then she adds, "This is very selfish of Mark."

"I'll let him know."

"And dragging you into it."

"I'll let him know."

Russ joins us, a plate full of pizza in his hand. "Can we get back to the movie now? I want to see Violet get tossed in the paddy wagon for being a ho."

❖ ❖ ❖

When I call Mark to tell him his mother has figured it out, I'm greeted with silence. Not steely silence or stony silence, more like stunned silence.

"Mark, are you there?"

I hear a soft "Yeah . . ."

"Well?"

"Well, what?"

"Are you going to call her?"

After another long moment he says, "I don't know. I don't think so. Not right away, anyway. No."

I hear Russ downstairs playing one of his video games, which is usually annoying, but right now it's a good thing — he can't be eavesdropping on my conversation on the upstairs phone. I say, "You're putting me in a really awkward position here. I don't want your mother coming by every day because you won't call her."

"Moll, you don't know the woman. I do. She's going to try and make me come back so she can change me. Don't you get it? She only wants me the way I was before I left, in the closet and miserable. And my dad . . ."

Russ must have lost his game, because from the sitting room I hear an electronic horn go *waah-waaaaaaah.*

I tell Mark, "Okay, sorry. But at least send her a card or something. You don't have to tell her where you're living."

He says, "You're right. I will. Moll, sorry about all this."

I say, "It's no biggie. What are friends for?"

I don't tell Simon, but Mark must have, because a couple of days later, I get an e-mail from Simon.

> Subject: Merry Third Day of Christmas (French hens not included)
>
> Spent the actual day with my folks on Long Island for our traditional Christmas Chinese dinner. I brought Mark out here today to try and cheer him up. We watched *The Elegant Universe* DVD, but he didn't seem particularly interested. I don't know how to get him out of this black hole he's in. Any ideas?
>
> S.
>
> P.S. The latest neutrinos report has been slammed by the supersymmetric particle camp.

I think about it. What would get Mark out of his funk? I reply:

Si-Man

I wouldn't try to cheer Mark up with M theory, it's just not his thing. Jim is a pig and he needs a new boyfriend. Mark told me he had his eye on someone new before I left for the break. Encourage him to go for it. Or get him a sketch pad and brainstorm some Mad Cow story lines. He needs to start submitting his work. I don't want him to work at Duane Reade forever (although I do enjoy the discounts).

Wish you were here. We could spend a day up in the Cities; I think you'd really like our Science Museum. It has a state-of-the-art IMAX theater and the building sits on the Mississippi River, which is beautiful to look out on from the balcony.

Love,

Molly

Yes, the "love" sign-off is taking a chance. But it can be read as romantic or simply affectionate. And I can mean it either way, too.

❖ ❖ ❖

Time, that unforgiving dimension, has taken a stubborn turn. It's only New Year's Eve but I feel as though months have passed since I got back. My social life consists of telling Russ and his burn-out friends about the music scene in New York (not that I'm an expert, but they are easily impressed), an occasional call to my old high school friend Maddie in the Cities (though we don't make any plans to see each other), and the near-daily e-mails and IMs to Simon and the Two *Es*. Mark seems to be missing in action, and I can't help but worry. I depend on Simon for updates about how Mark is doing.

So with all this free time to ponder, I ask Jessie's and Lily's advice about whether it's too soon to sleep with Simon. Lily wants to know if I'm in love with him while Jessie wonders if Simon is putting undue pressure on me because I'm a virgin.

I write Lily that I think I might be in love and I write Jessie that Simon is not that kind of guy. Lily writes back that if I don't know if I'm in love or not then I'm not and it is too soon. Jessie writes back that *all guys are that kind of guy.*

I would talk about it with Mom if the subject

wouldn't make her head explode. I don't know why losing your virginity is such a big deal. Well, that's not true, it is a big deal. A very big deal, and part of what makes it such a big deal is all the pressure on you to do it or not do it.

I wonder if I would be having these doubts if Mark were straight and my boyfriend.

Actually, I wonder if I would be having these doubts if Mark were just straight.

Anyway, tonight Mom and I are staying up late to ring in the new year. Russ is at a party with his friends, and Dad is on the road (of course), so that leaves the two Swain women on their own. True, we did get invitations from Mom's sisters to spend the night with them, but Mom doesn't like sleeping in a strange bed and she refuses to drive anywhere on New Year's Eve because of "all the drunks on the road."

So here we are, drinking pink champagne and trying to stay awake.

And it's only 10:30 P.M. (11:30 P.M. EST).

Mom says, "You probably wish you were at Times Square right about now."

"Not really. That's too crowded even for me. It would be nice to be with Simon, though. I miss him."

"The boyfriend," Mom says with relief. "The *real* boyfriend."

"Why does that sound like another swipe at Mark?"

"Sorry," she mutters, and then louder says, "So tell me about this Simon. All I've heard about him is that he loves something called matrix theory, is Jewish, and lives on Long Island. Oh, and that he can press two hundred pounds. So what are you *not* telling me?"

"Nothing!"

"He doesn't have a pierced nose or a tattoo on his face, does he?"

"Of course not." Then I add, "Maybe there is one thing I haven't told you about him."

She squints at me. "What?"

"He's on antidepressants. Or he was."

Mom de-squints. "So's your aunt Aggie. I was on them myself awhile after your uncle Tim died."

I take a sip of my champagne, glad that Mom felt she could share that with me. I'm about to say something profound when I humiliate myself by burping.

Mom says, "That's attractive. You're becoming more like your father every day." She runs a hand through her hair, which has gotten even longer, past her shoulders and white as the snow we still don't have. Next she dabs a potato chip in ranch dip, saying, "I need to eat or the bubbly is gonna make me drunk."

By 11:17 P.M., Mom has fallen asleep in Dad's La-Z-Boy and is snoring softly. Since we finished the bottle of André pink champagne, I head to the kitchen for a beer. Normally, I'm not a big drinker, but this is such a depressing way to spend New Year's Eve, I feel like I should have a Pabst.

At 11:30 the phone rings and I'm thrilled: It's Lily and Jessie. Lily is in Grosse Pointe and Jessie is in San Francisco, but they arranged a conference call. I gush, "I miss you guys so much!"

Lily says, "We miss you, too! We weren't sure we'd find you home. Doesn't Le Sueur have the largest out-door celebration after Times Square?"

"Funny," I tell her. "Very funny."

Lily says, "At least you're not in Grosse Pointe. My parents are at the yacht club for a private fireworks display, and I've eaten an entire tub of Farmer Jack's French onion dip by myself."

"You're not at a party?" I imagined she'd be at some party.

She says, "I'm heading out soon. I wait until after midnight because I don't want some loser kissing me."

Jessie says, "Chris called to wish me a Happy New Year!"

Lily and I grunt noncommittally. Then Jessie says, "And some of my high school crowd are going to Japantown for dinner. What are you up to tonight, Molly?"

I say, "Well, my mom fell asleep in the La-Z-Boy, and I'm having one of my dad's beers."

Lily says, "You party animal!"

"So what's Nathan doing for New Year's Eve?" Jessie asks.

"Lighting candles in front of a picture of me," Lily replies with a sigh. "He's been calling way too much. I think he's in love with me."

"Why do you say that?" I ask.

"Because he called to tell me that he was in love with me."

Jessie says, "Oh. What did you say?"

"You know me, Ms. Sensitive. I said, 'That's nice.' Then I pretended that my mom needed the phone."

"You could do a lot worse," I point out.

Lily sighs again. "I just feel awful. We have so much in common and he's really a sweet guy. But doesn't it seem a bit soon for the *L* word?"

Jessie says, "If Chris told me that, I'd be so happy I don't know what I'd do."

Lily asks, "So what's Simon doing tonight?"

"Spending it with his parents," I reply.

Jessie asks, "So you gonna let him pop your cherry or what?"

Lily interrupts. "Don't be so crass. Molly has to be sure that the time is right for her and that this is the right guy."

Jessie snorts. "You sound like a sex ed class."

I hear myself say: "I think I'm ready."

They say in unison: "Really?"

"Is anyone ever one-hundred-percent sure?"

We talk until midnight my time and wish one another a happy new year. As I hang up I want to cry, I miss the Two *E*s so much. I pick up the phone again and call Simon at his parents' house. It's his mother who answers, and she sounds like I woke her up. When I apologize she just says, "Please, it's lovely to hear your voice."

"Is Simon still up?"

She laughs. "Oh, Simon stayed in the city. At the last minute he and his roommate decided to go to Times Square. How's your family?"

"Dad's on the road, my brother's at a party, and my mom's asleep. She couldn't make it till midnight."

"A woman after my own heart. You have a happy New Year's, Molly."

"Thanks. You, too."

I try Simon and Mark to wish them a happy new year, but all I get is voice mail.

I wish I were there with them. So much it hurts.

JANUARY

R uss rang in the new year by losing his virginity.
I know this because the upstairs phone is just
outside my bedroom.

He can't wait to call one of his loser friends and tell
him about his hookup. He says, "Oh my God, dude, it
was . . . oh my God."

I rub my eyes (it's not even seven A.M.) and get up
and open my bedroom door. I whisper hoarsely, "Russ,
keep your voice down. Mom'll hear."

He tells the phone, "I feel . . . different, you know. It
was sooo awesome."

I wonder who the girl is. Whoever is on the other
end of the phone is wondering the same thing, too.

Russ says, "Her name's Lynn and she goes to
Mankato West." He can barely contain himself when he
whispers, "She's a *senior*!"

I ask, "Was she drunk?"

Russ puts his hand over the receiver and tells me
matter-of-factly, "Yeah. We both were." He turns his

attention back to the phone and says, "Gotta go, dude. Just wanted you to be the first to know." He hangs up with a big goofy grin on his face.

I fold my arms across my chest and ask, "Are you going to see her again?"

"Oh yeah. She's all that and a bag of chips! I'm gonna see all of her again and again, you know what I mean?"

"Russ, please. I'm your sister, not one of your drinking buddies. Did you use protection?"

"You mean like a condom?"

I shoot a look at Mom's bedroom door. "Not so loud! And no, not 'like a condom.' An actual condom."

He hangs his head, but only a little. "Didn't have any, Molly-Pop."

Oh no. "Tell me she's on the pill."

"Didn't ask."

I smack him on the back of his head and he says, "Hey!"

"*You didn't ask?* Why not?"

"I thought she might, you know, stop. I didn't want her to stop."

Men.

I mean, *Boys.*

Russ says, "It was all like, really —"

"Okay, stop talking *now.*"

"I've only ever gotten to second base before and —"

I stick my fingers in my ears and sing *la la la*. Then I sing, "This is me, not listening." Then I sing *la la la* some more.

When I'm done, Russ looks at me seriously. "Okay, I'll get some condoms."

"Good."

He frowns now. "Have you and Simon . . . ?"

"No! And besides, that's none of your business!"

He heads to his bedroom to finally get some sleep, saying, "Okay, okay. Sorry I asked."

So it's finally official. Everyone on the planet has had sex except me. But instead of feeling embarrassed, I feel a little proud of myself. I understand that sex is a natural biological urge, but at the same time, I don't want to be anyone's hookup or one-nighter.

I head back to my room, and as the sky becomes brighter, I pick up a paper and pen. I haven't done this in years.

Resolutions for the New Year
 1. Eat healthier and lose five pounds.
 2. Exercise every other day.
 3. Budget more time for studying.
 4. Do a better job of saving money.

5. Read all the assigned texts; don't just look up the synopsis on the Web.
6. Treat people the way I would like to be treated, no matter how big of a jerk they are.
7. Be a better daughter and call home more often.
8. Be a good friend to Mark.
9. Be a good friend to Jessie and Lily.
10. Be a good girlfriend to Simon. Be more patient with his nerd-ier impulses. Don't try to change him, just accept him as he is.
11. Once you've accepted him as he is, <u>then</u> try to change him.

I consider starting with resolution eight by calling Mark and reminding him to write a letter to his mother, but that could be seen as nagging, and if I am to be a good friend, I shouldn't nag.

Oh, what the heck? One friendly little call won't hurt.

But all I get is the answering machine.

Dad has been hovering since he got home, which is unlike him. Usually, he pops open a PBR and reclines with the remote in his non-beer-drinking hand, but today he wants to spend time with me, doing what he calls "father–daughter stuff." When I ask him what sort of stuff that is, a blank expression comes over his face. He finally says, "How about dinner and a movie, just the two of us?" Mom has to work and Russ is with his senior from Mankato West, so there's no one to exclude anyway.

At The Bar on Main, Dad orders a beer and a burger while I have a salad and a diet pop. After the waitress leaves, he says, "You eat anything but rabbit food anymore?"

I tell him, "Just trying to watch my weight."

He scratches his brown-and-gray hair, and I notice it's gotten thinner. He says, "Don't lose too much. A lot of gals your age have those eating disorders. Waste away to nothing."

I still need to lose five pounds. I say, "No worries."

When the drinks arrive, he proposes a toast to his Sweet Pea. He says, "To you, Molly Katherine Swain, girl genius. You make me proud."

I say, "Thanks, Dad."

He talks about the new Environmental Protection Agency's emissions regulations that mandate exhaust after-treatment for diesel rigs. He says, "Diesel filters are going to need serious maintenance. Seems the costs of doing business just keep going up and up."

I say, "That's good, though. I mean, with global warming it's good to reduce emissions."

He says, "You can reduce the soot from the exhaust pipe, and you can cure the NOx. But it's next to impossible to do both at the same time. Cure one and you make the other worse."

I take a sip of my diet pop. Now I know how he feels when I talk about string theory.

He says, "And they're adding tolls all the time. It costs eighteen bucks just to drive seven miles of express lane on Colorado I-25. Everybody thinks truckers are made of money. Well, guess what, we aren't."

I say, "Sorry, Dad."

When our food arrives, he says, "So you're happy out there in New York?"

I say, "You know I am."

He chews his gigantic burger slowly, deliberately, and then he swallows. When he can speak he says, "I just meant now that you're back home again. I thought maybe spending time back here might make you want to stay."

I look at him, the shy but hopeful look in his eyes. He wants me to be a success, but he doesn't want me living so far away to do it. He's proud of me living in New York and worried about me living in New York. I say, "I'll be back for the summer."

He dips a fry in mayonnaise, a taste he developed when he was snowed in outside of Fargo. He says, "It's not the same. Not having you home . . . it just feels like the whole world has been turned upside down. When I'm on the road, it's easy to pretend you're home. When I pull up, I still expect to see you."

I smile as I stare at my salad. I really wanted a burger. I say, "I know it's hard to get used to."

He laughs sadly. "You seem to be used to it. Guess I'll just have to get used to it, too. My little Sweet Pea is all grown up. I remember when I held you in my arms for the first time —"

I groan. "Dad . . ."

He picks up another fry as he says, "When you have children of your own, you'll understand."

I stab a tomato wedge. "I'll take your word for that."

He smiles at me. Then the smile disappears. He says,

"The price of gas is gonna put me out of business, Sweet Pea. And the freight companies are bleeding me dry. Seems like I just work so I can pay for gas so I can work." He takes a swig of beer. "Sorry, didn't mean to dump all this on you. I've just been worrying a lot."

"I think you spend all your time on the road worrying. I wish you wouldn't."

He repeats himself: "When you have children of your own, you'll understand."

Soon enough, my time in Le Sueur is at an end, and as much as I complained about being bored, I don't want to leave Mom and Dad and Russ. It's finally snowing when they drive me to the Lindbergh Terminal, and I insist they just drop me off curbside, so they won't be stuck in bad weather. I'm almost two hours early for my flight (because Dad worries). They all get out of the car to say their good-byes.

Mom gives me a big hug and reminds me to call *the very second* I get to my room.

Dad gives me a big hug and tells me to *be careful out there*.

Russ, who has a date tonight with the Mankato West senior who puts out, gives me a big hug and tells me to *stay full of grooviness.*

And they're off, and I'm relieved and sad and excited all at the same time.

On the plane, I imagine Simon waiting for me at LaGuardia, picturing the brown hair, the ears that stick out a little, the intense look in his eyes when he speculates about M theory, his holy grail. I miss him.

When I surface in the LaGuardia terminal, Simon is right there as I imagined. He waves and shouts, "Molly, over here!"

There's a formulation in quantum physics called sum-over-paths in which particles travel from one location to another along all possible paths between them. This is how Simon and I head toward each other, along all possible paths, until he wraps me up in his arms and says, "Welcome home!"

Welcome home, Molly Swain. Welcome home to New York. Welcome home to Simon.

And I kiss him, right there in LaGuardia Airport. Yes, he has to work on his social skills. Yes, he worries too much, even more than I do and perhaps more than my dad does. True, our relationship is still very new to both of us. But when he lifts me in the air with those strong arms as if I were as light as a bouquet, I *know* I'm in love. With him, with this city, with my life here.

Simon pulls away and I blush. That's when I notice Mark standing at a distance, not far from a crowd of young tourists speaking French. He says, "Hey, Moll! Welcome back!" He looks good, but then he always does, and whatever lust I may have felt for him melts away into genuine friendship. (Okay, there's still a bit of lust that refuses to melt.) When we embrace, the urge to dip him and kiss him right on the lips is gone. Finally. He's my friend, I'm his, and this seems to be enough. In fact, it feels completely right.

On the ride back to the city, I sit next to Simon as Mark stares out the window from the backseat. Mark asks about Le Sueur now and then, and I can tell that, in spite of himself, he's a little homesick. He refuses to ask the question I know he most wants to ask: *How's my mom and dad doing?* Maybe it's because Simon's with us, maybe it's because he's afraid of what I'll say.

Simon, on the other hand, is far from silent, and finally it's not about quantum mechanics. "Times Square was awesome!" he tells me. "I've never done New Year's Eve in the city! It was amazing, all the people partying right in the streets! We had *such* a good time."

As Simon talks about his exploits with Mark in the

city, I realize I've gotten everyone a gift except Mark. As they drop me off at the dorm, I give Simon a little stuffed wolf and gifts for his parents, and he gives me a kiss before he and Mark leave.

Mark tells me he wants to get together, just the two of us. We make a date for tomorrow.

There's a wonderful sight awaiting me at JJ: The Two *E*s have decorated my door with a big WELCOME BACK, QUANTUM QUEEN banner. Underneath they've superimposed a picture of Brian Greene next to a picture of me, and it looks like we're a couple out on a date. They've also added dialogue balloons:

Brian Greene: *I love you for your branes, not your body!*

Me: *Oh, Professor Greene, show me your superstring!*

The Three *E*s convene in Lily's room and drink from the Last Refuge of the Damned. When I comment on all the flowers on her desk, Lily just says, "Nathan overdid it. Again."

I present them with their gifts: For Lily there's a black beret and sunglasses like film directors wear, and for Jessie a book of blonde jokes to encourage her to keep growing her hair out instead of touching up the roots, which she is considering doing. Lily gives me a *Physics Workshop: The Science of Matter and Energy* play set for ages 8–12. She says, "Look, it has over three hundred pieces and fun, easy-to-follow directions!"

Jessie gives me a Holiday Barbie, adding, "I just couldn't help myself."

And so it goes, the Three *E*s talking the night away while Holiday Barbie watches from inside her box, her arms and legs bound into position with twist ties.

Mark and I meet the next day at Columbus Circle. For our official reunion, we decide on a coffee shop in a bookstore — once Mark has finished looking at "art books" full of black-and-white photos of buff men in various stages of undress. I'm sure he'd buy a few if his job at Duane Reade paid more.

The other people in the shop are reading or text-messaging or working on laptops so Mark is careful to keep his voice down — afraid, I guess, that people will overhear us talking about where we come from and who he is. After he takes a sip of coffee drowned in cream and sugar, he asks in his soft voice, "So, did they decorate Main for the holidays?"

"Youbetcha."

"Did you see anyone from high school?"

I grimace. "Donna Piambino. Guess what: She's pregnant and Thirsty Dave is the father. They're getting married in June so her *little angel* can be in the wedding."

Mark laughs and asks for more news about our classmates, which I can't provide since, well, I wasn't exactly Miss Popularity at our high school. He asks if my family went to the Holiday Parade (our town's annual march down Main Street) and if the Valleygreen Square Mall was decked out for the holidays. I say, "I don't know. I went to the Mall of America to shop."

He frowns. "You should really support the local economy."

I can't help it — I smirk. "*The local economy?* You didn't even come back for Christmas!"

"Yeah, like I *could* go back."

I shake my head. "Of course you could. Jeez, Mark, you act like a refugee. I'm sure your mom and dad —"

"Don't," he tells me. "Don't go there."

But I do, anyway. "Your mom really wants to see you."

He lets out a sigh and tells me he has to get to work.

"We just got here," I protest.

But he downs his coffee and leaves.

That night, Mark's out and Simon and I are finally alone together, in his apartment with soft Dixie Chicks music (I brought some CDs) and aromatic candles (yes, I brought those, too). In other words, I'm prepared for whatever might happen. (It was mortifying, but I bought some condoms at one of the ten thousand Duane Reade stores that Mark does not work at.)

Simon holds me as we lie on his bed, and his arms feel even bigger and stronger than before. I rest my head on his shoulder as he strokes my hair. I look up at him and lean in to kiss him.

And we make out and we make out and we make out.

And I know I'm in love.

I whisper to Simon, "I'm ready."

Simon asks, "For what?"

I can't help it, I'm so nervous: I giggle a little. I say, "You know. For . . . that. You know."

And Simon leans on an elbow and looks at me for a

long moment, his face flushed. Finally, he whispers, "I don't think we should."

Oh.

I sit up.

I don't think I've ever been more embarrassed in my entire life. This is all Russ's fault. Just because he lost his virginity doesn't mean I have to. I could just *kill* him.

Simon says, "Molly, don't get upset."

I feel like crying, I'm so humiliated. And I hear myself say, "Why? Just because I'm fat and ugly and no man would ever want me? I shouldn't get upset over a little thing like that?"

He closes his eyes and says softly, "Molly . . . I just don't think it's the right time."

I pout and mutter, "Maybe I do."

"I thought you wanted to wait until you were married."

I did say that. But now I say, "That was the plan. But plans can change. Can't they?"

He says, "I think your original plan is still the best one."

What is wrong with this guy? What is wrong with me? I ask, more confused than humiliated now, "Why? Why is the original plan still the best?"

I resist a little as he pulls me back down into his arms. But then I lay my head on his chest. He says, "Because it's the right thing. You're not fat, and you're not ugly, and any man in his right mind would want you. I just think it's the right thing to wait." Then he squeezes me tightly and asks softly, "Isn't this enough?"

No.

Yes.

Molly Swain, you're an idiot on an astronomical scale. His arms around me, the sound of his heartbeat, this should be more than enough. I say, "Of course. I'm sorry."

And now I really, really know I'm in love. Yes, it's sappy, but I want us to wait for our wedding night. Just holding him, being held by him, this is enough. Just because everyone else on the planet is in the fast lane doesn't mean Simon and I have to be.

It's not like the sun shines through the window of the apartment to let us know that a new day has dawned. It's almost brighter in Simon's place at night when the streetlights are on. But just like in Le Sueur, the birds are singing, and though it's still early, I sit up in bed and look down at Simon, who's sleeping in the fetal position, his crooked lips open, his dramatic eyebrows frowning just a little bit. I stare at him, wondering what life would be like with him as my husband. Would we stay in New York? Would he get some prestigious job with a research university? Would I? Would we stay in New York or move to some European capital? Would we have children?

I'm getting ahead of myself.

I lean under the bed and slide out the box of comic books, picking up a copy of *Hawkman*, a superhero with wings and a beak mask who doesn't wear a shirt. I try, but I just can't get into it, so I admire the art, the way the muscular men and gi-normously breasted women try to beat the crap out of one another. And then I decide it's time for some coffee, a bad habit that I think is unavoidable if you're in college.

In the tiny kitchen area, I see Mark leisurely pouring water into the coffeepot as he adjusts the band of his boxers, the only piece of clothing he has on. His brown summer skin has faded, replaced with a clear, pale tone that doesn't reveal a single blemish. When he senses my presence, he turns, but he doesn't smile. He just says, "Hey, Moll."

I say, "Good morning." He must be waiting for me to tell him to call his mother, but I don't.

Simon joins us with a mumbled "hello" as we wait for the coffee to brew. He stares at Mark as he leans against a counter and I look at Simon, my face trying to tell him not to be rude, I'm not comparing him to Mark.

Before the coffee's even done, Mark mutters "excuse me" and heads to the bathroom.

I tell Simon, "I'm really glad we talked last night. I think we're right to wait."

Simon smiles with his crooked lips before he says, "I think we're right, too."

I pour us some coffee as Mark emerges, fully dressed, from the bathroom. As soon as he hits the kitchen, he says, "Gotta go."

"At this hour?" I ask.

He nods and leaves without saying good-bye, like he couldn't wait to get out of here. And then it dawns on me: He's not waiting for me to nag him about his mother. He thinks Simon and I have gone all the way.

What else *would* he think? Here I am with Simon after having spent the night. I want to go after Mark, set him straight — so to speak — but it will have to wait.

Right now I just want to be with Simon.

FEBRUARY

The new semester is, amazingly, going to be more work than the last one, if the syllabi are to be believed. I'm still stuck with requirements, but at last I'll actually get to hear Brian Greene speak: He's going to guest-lecture at my Frontiers of Science class in April. I wonder if he'll be as wonderful in person as he was in *The Elegant Universe* series. I look at his author photo on the back of *The Fabric of the Cosmos*. He's smiling at the camera, an ocean behind him. I wonder how tall he is. I wonder if his thick brown hair is now peppered with gray.

Okay, check yourself, Molly. You admire the man's *mind*. His *ideas*. His *theories*.

And besides, he's too old for you.

Really, my obsession with Brian Greene is not my problem this semester. My problem is that I truly just enjoy hanging out with Simon and my friends too much.

When I received the news of my acceptance to Columbia last spring I was ecstatic and had every intention of being the model student, a protégée of Brian Greene. And while in principle I appreciate the reasoning behind the core curriculum, in practice I find it tedious, which must be why I just want to hang out with Simon and my friends and have fun.

The other motivation for slacking off could be the fact that I never slacked off in high school, because, well, I never had a reason or the opportunity. Slacking off would have only emphasized the fact that I had virtually no one to slack off *with*, so studying occupied the time that would have otherwise reminded me that I was a very lonely person.

I find it ironic that I had to be awarded a full scholarship and be admitted to a prestigious New York school to discover that, under the right circumstances, I can be just as lazy and unmotivated as everybody else.

Like now. It's two weeks into the semester, and I take a deep breath and try to highlight what I hope are the important sections in my textbook, but frankly, I'm just waiting for Simon. He spends a few nights each week with me in my room — never the apartment — and we lie on my bed holding each other as we read.

And now, here he is. I left the door open so he could come in and lie down next to me. He pulls me into his arms and I give up on the book that I'm supposed to have read for class tomorrow. I say, "Good day?"

He grunts. "A long day. And yet, not long enough. I've got so much to do."

I close my eyes and savor the feel of him next to me. I say, "Me, too."

He asks, "How are Lily and Jessie?"

I smile with my eyes closed and run a hand through his hair. "They're either asleep, in class, or studying. How's Mark?"

"What do you mean?"

I open my eyes and look at his profile, his eyes shut, his lips slightly open. I say, "I mean, how's he doing?"

"Oh, Mark is Mark," he says, annoyed.

While I haven't told Simon all the details about how Mark and I came to be friends — e.g., the fact that I was in love with him — Simon must have clued in by now. But if I tell him I'm not in love with Mark anymore, he'll probably wonder why I felt the need to tell him. It's silly, really. There's no reason to be jealous of a gay guy.

I play with the collar of Simon's shirt, but he just shakes his head and says he has a lot of reading to do.

Days pass, spent trying to read, to comprehend, and to demonstrate comprehension. In other words, the Three *Es* need to blow off some steam. To celebrate Valentine's Day, we — Simon, me, Lily, Nathan, Jessie, Maybe-Chris (as Lily and I now refer to him, since he never confirms anything with Jessie), and Mark — are going to a retro roller disco in Chelsea that plays disco hits of the seventies. Lily thought of it, and she took Jessie and me on a field trip to a secondhand clothing store on the Lower East Side to look for suitable attire. The guys were left to their own devices and, therefore, look like they always do.

The Three *Es*, however, are *foxy ladies.* There was an abundance of spandex and headbands at the store Lily took us to, so we're outfitted in black spandex pants (Lily, Jessie) and pink spandex pants (me). We all wear green headbands and thick blue eye shadow along with bright print polyester blouses opened to our cleavage, and as many necklaces as we can wear and still be able to stand upright. Lily found a spectacularly ugly fake-gold rope necklace with a tiny treasure chest hanging from it, which actually opens. She put baby powder in the chest and we pretend to take hits of cocaine from it.

It's the seventies, after all.

The guys are slightly embarrassed by us (except for Maybe-Chris, who isn't here but might still show up), but this is *ladies' night and the feeling's right!* The fact that none of us can really roller-skate doesn't prove to be the obstacle you might think it would be.

The roller disco is small with a disco ball that sends beads of bright light in every direction. We're discussing technique just outside the rink when a song comes on and Jessie screams, "I LOVE THIS SONG!"

She grabs my hand and, before I know it, we're circling the rink as best we can while she sings along with the music: *If I can't have you, I don't want nobody, baby.*

I shout at her, "How do you know this song?"

She shouts back, ecstatic, "My father played it when I was growing up! He loves Yvonne Elliman!"

Inspired by us, Lily and Nathan shakily take the ring, followed by Simon and Mark. Couples speed by us as they spin and twirl each other, and there's a group of gay men, a few years older than us, who lip-sync and do hand motions as they effortlessly skate by. One of their group, a tall guy who wears a tank top and very short cut-off jeans to show off his muscular, shaved legs, points right at Mark on the chorus and lip-syncs: *If I can't have you.* You have to love New York, where every-one feels free, gay or straight, to flirt with the best-looking guy in the room. Mark himself seems flat-tered, but his concentration is focused on staying vertical. Simon, on the other hand, shoots disapproving looks at the gay men.

So he's still a bit uptight. I'll work on that.

Jessie and I are laughing as she tries to spin me, and I fall flat on my butt. That's when Simon appears and says, "May I cut in?"

Jessie is laughing too hard to speak, which Simon takes as a yes.

I hold out my hand, still laughing. "Help me up."

He pulls me up, nearly falling over himself.

We put one arm around each other's waist and try to steady ourselves with the other. A new song comes on, and we hear, *Don't you leave me this wa-ay.*

We make steady progress as the other couples and gay men zip past us, some of them passing two or three times in the time it takes us to get around once.

On his third pass, I'm surprised to see the gay guy with the short-shorts with his arm around Mark as they slowly make their way, their strides in time. Short-shorts is trying to teach Mark the finer points, and as they roll in front of us I'm a bit shocked to see Mark's hand firmly in Short-shorts' back pocket.

I look at Simon and say, "Mark's a fast worker."

But Simon just scowls at them, and I realize again how much I take for granted that I can walk with Simon hand in hand without worrying about being straight-bashed. It makes me feel bad for Mark.

But mostly, I'm worried. Short-shorts reminds me of Jim, and we all know how *that* turned out. And the moment I think about Mark and Jim, I fall flat on my ass.

Simon leans down and offers me his hand, asking "Are you okay?"

"I'm fine. Sometimes having a butt as big as an air-bag has its advantages. It cushions the impact."

He steadies me as he says, "Don't talk about yourself like that. You're beautiful."

Sometimes he knows exactly what to say. We reposition ourselves as Mark and Short-shorts pass us by yet again. This time Short-shorts kisses the top of Mark's head and Mark laughs.

I sigh. "Guess he's over Jim now."

Simon grunts. "Of course. He'll flirt with anybody."

Anybody except me.

We carefully make our way to the concession stand where Jessie is sipping on a diet Coke as she stares at the doors, hoping, no doubt, that Maybe-Chris will still show up. Every now and then she checks her cell phone to make sure it's still on.

Simon orders a hot dog, and I can't help myself — I wonder if it's kosher. I want to ask, but I don't really know what kosher means, and I don't know if Simon is kosher anyway. Note to self: Learn more about Jews.

Mark joins us now, flushed and out of breath. He's unbuttoned his shirt and his smooth chest is glowing like the rest of him. He says, "I got his phone number!"

Jessie asks, "You mean the guy with the legs?"

Mark nods, ecstatic. He says, "He's a police cadet! Isn't that cool?"

Simon says, "Sure he is."

But Mark doesn't pay any attention. He says, "He wants to be a homicide detective one day!"

Well, maybe this guy is worth Mark's time. I'd feel better knowing that he was out in the city with someone who knows how to defend himself.

Simon, however, isn't impressed. All he says is, "Don't bring strangers back to the apartment."

Mark shoots him a look and says, "No one could be stranger than *you*."

Lily and Nathan join us now, while the gay Sherlock Holmes in short-shorts hovers near us on the rink, waiting for Mark's return. Before Mark goes back to his cadet, he pulls little sealed envelopes out of his back pocket, saying, "Here, I almost forgot." He hands one to Lily, Jessie, and me, and when we open them, we discover they're valentines, the kind that you used to bring to class in elementary school. Mine has a picture of Scooby-Doo being kissed on the cheeks by Daphne and Velma.

Nathan makes a little joke: "Don't Simon and I get one?"

Mark laughs, but Simon doesn't think it's funny.

I, however, am touched that Mark was thoughtful enough to give the Three *E*s valentines. Yes, they were most likely stolen from Duane Reade, but as Mom says, *It's the thought that counts.* And after the broody-but-adorable Mark I knew back in Le Sueur, I find the happy-yet-unattainable Mark I know in New York a change for the better.

Mark heads back to the rink to skate with Officer Short-shorts and the rest of us follow as Rod Stewart asks the musical question *Do ya think I'm sexy?* Nathan and Lily are fearless now, trying out dance steps only to topple over again and again. Simon and I just set our own pace, nearly falling backward, nearly falling face-first, but hanging on to each other so if one of us goes down, the other will too.

Call me naive, or perhaps a bit smug having been valedictorian, but I had no idea that college would be so much work. I mean, I knew it would be hard, but *come on.* There are only so many hours in the day, and it seems like my professors expect me to give up showering, eating, and sleeping in order to keep up with the books and papers they assign. When I go to Simon's apartment, we grunt our hellos, boil some noodles, open our books, and highlight what seems important as we down empty calories. I always hope Mark will be there to distract me since Simon seems so tired lately, and, frankly, a bit crabby. Due to our workload, I guess.

But Mark is never around: He's always at work or with his police cadet, and if I didn't know any better, I would say he was avoiding me. But then, if I were him, I would avoid me, too. I mean, there's nothing more boring than an overachiever who is dating an overachiever, who, when together, spend their time overachieving.

Still, I wish there were more time; when I look at the clock thinking minutes have passed, it's hours instead. I tell myself not to pay attention to time anymore, that unforgiving dimension, because all it does is remind me of how much more I have to do.

MARCH

Dad always says that youth is wasted on the young, but I think youth is wasted on term papers, midterms, and research projects. If these are supposed to be the best years of my life, I demand a refund. I was supposed to go to Simon's tonight, but he's so stressed about school that he told me not to bother. It's the closest we've come so far to having a fight.

So I'm in my room at JJ, forcing myself to catch up with my reading.

And yet, the vending machines beckon me.

As I walk down the hall I see Chris emerge from Jessie's room. He smiles, says, "Hey, Millie."

"Molly."

"Hey, Molly. Good to see you. Have a great day!"

And then, like a candidate late for his next fundraiser, he's gone.

I knock tentatively on Jessie's door. I hear her ask, "Chris?"

I open the door a little and peek my head in. "Just me. Sorry."

She waves me in from where she lies in her bed, a sheet pulled up to her armpits. Her face looks flushed. I sit at the end of her bed and say, "So. What's new?"

She smiles slightly and says, "Don't worry, I don't embarrass easily. So you caught me ATB, big deal."

ATB is an acronym for **A**fter **T**he **B**ang. In physics it refers to the time that has passed since the Big Bang. The reversal of the Big Bang is called the Big Crunch, when the expanding universe stops expanding and collapses in on itself. If the Big Crunch theory turns out to be true, it won't happen for trillions of years.

But I think Jessie's personal Big Crunch is imminent. I say, "I saw Chris on his way out. He called me Millie."

Jessie says, "Oh, *that's* nothing. Want to know what he called *me* about ten minutes ago?"

"What did he . . . oh."

"Lisa! Do you know any Lisas?"

I shake my head.

She sighs. "I'm like, 'Who's Lisa?' You should have seen the look on his face."

I give her ankle a little shake and say, "Sorry."

She looks at me seriously. "Molly, am I a ho?"

I shake my head. "No. But your boyfriend is."

She rubs her eyes. "You know what I think? I think I could use a boy-free zone for a while."

This was supposed to be a night out for all of us. But Lily isn't in the mood to spend time with Nathan and Jessie has decided not to come, to teach Maybe-Chris a lesson. But he's a no-show, so he will have to learn his lesson some other time.

So it's just the three of us, Simon, Mark, and me. And maybe it's the claustrophobia of sharing a tiny Washington Heights apartment, or maybe it's the pressure of studying, but they seem mad at each other, too.

Our tense trio is sitting at a table in a Cuban restaurant on the West Side. Mark is on his second beer, I'm still nursing my glass of white wine, and Simon, who usually doesn't drink, is halfway through a margarita.

After explaining why no one else is coming, I sit quietly between them as they glare at each other. I say meekly, "Something wrong?"

Simon says, "Ask your friend who doesn't know how to wash a dish. As fast as I can kill the roaches, he's feeding them. They're not birds, Mark — you don't have to set out feeders for them."

Mark takes a long sip of beer.

Simon says, "Did you know, Molly, that there are these wonderful machines that you put dirty clothes in and then — poof! — like magic, they're clean. They keep these wonderful machines in a place the natives call a *Laundromat*. Of course, you could always just leave your dirty clothes lying around everywhere and hope that somehow they'll clean themselves, but my sources tell me that these washing machines work even better."

I drink some more white wine.

Mark says, "This guy is always on my case lately, I mean always."

Simon grumbles something I can't make out. When he does speak up he says, "And you, Mark, are inertia personified. You are the property of an object that resists being accelerated. No, no, I'm sorry, I'm wrong. You're *dark matter*. You exert gravity but shine no light."

I say, "Simon, come on. Mark's your friend, remember?"

Mark looks at his beer, pretending to be wounded. "Gosh. Physics insults. Stop it before I cry, you big loser."

I say, "Mark!"

Simon shoots back, "You want to see a loser, look in the mirror. Oh, wait, you always have your face in a mirror before you head out with your police rookie who loves Mark and has to call 24/7. I can't study with your cell phone going off every five minutes. Tell your cop to have a doughnut and stop calling all the time."

"Simon!"

The couple at the table next to us is unkindly glancing our way.

Mark says, "You're just pissed because the only people who call you are your mommy and daddy." To me, Mark says, "You should hear him, the perfect little boy saying all the right things to his perfect parents."

I say, "That's not funny. Simon's parents are wonderful people."

Simon huffs, "You know, Mark, three's a crowd."

Mark shoots Simon a look of pure contempt. He looks like he's about to say something but thinks better of it.

Okay, I'm done. I say, "You're right, Simon. I'm out of here."

They both look at me in shock.

I stand, saying, "I mean it! God, there's more important things than who does the dishes and who does the laundry."

Simon says, "I'm sorry, Molly."

Mark says, "Sorry, Moll."

I sit back down, but just barely. I say, "Now shake hands and apologize."

They look at each other uncertainly. Since I'm sitting between them, Simon stretches his arm in front of me, saying, "Sorry, Inert Dark Matter."

Mark takes his hand, shakes it, and says, "No problem, ya Loser-slash-Nerd-slash-Geek."

I suppose you could call it a first step.

The evening goes by quietly as we eat our food. My small talk falls on deaf ears. Mark stares into space and Simon keeps looking at him, waiting for him to really apologize. After we pay the check, Mark heads out to meet his police cadet, telling Simon *not to wait up, Mommy.* Instead of spending the night in my room, Simon just drops me off at JJ, giving me a quick kiss good night.

I call Simon the next day to apologize (for what, I'm not sure), but all I get is his voice mail.

I'm desperately trying to catch up on my reading when, alert to any distraction, *any* thing that might serve as an excuse to set my books aside, I hear muffled voices being raised from next door. Lily and Nathan are having a fight, and not their first.

I make out Lily: "You're suffocating me!"

I make out Nathan: "I'm sorry, I don't mean to. Just tell me what to do and I'll do it!"

Lily: "Do you hear yourself? Nate, you have to back off. I like you, but come on, I can't take it anymore."

They move out of overhearing range, and I wonder if I'm doing what Nathan is doing, smothering the object of my affection. I need to give Simon more space, stop calling him every day. But he hasn't complained about it.

Yet.

I hear the sound of Nathan as he leaves, his regret almost audible. Am I being a caring friend or a nosy neighbor? I step out in the hall and knock softly on Lily's door.

I say, "It's Molly."

"Come on in."

She's sitting on her bed, a Kleenex in her folded hands. But she's not crying. She has a resigned expression on her face, as if she had witnessed something that would have happened no matter what she had done to try to prevent it.

I sit next to her. I tell her, "Sounded bad."

She looks at me, shaking her head. "Nate's a nice guy. But he covers me like a second skin. I try to be polite — I know, *me, polite* — and it only encourages him. Believe it or not, I hate confrontation. I hate it when anyone is mad at me. I guess that's why I let this simmer for so long. I mean, I want to see what's out there, you know? Nate'll be awesome for someone someday, but not for me, and not now."

I give her a squeeze.

She says, "You know what the worst part of it is? Hurting him. Knowing what I'll say will hurt him, and then watching my words do exactly that. This is my fault, I should have seen it coming."

I assure her, "It's not your fault."

She looks to me like she hasn't slept in a week. She says, "All the signs were there, I just didn't bother to read them. I was too busy being flattered." I look at her as she runs a hand through her hair. She says, "You know what? Jessie's right about needing a boy-free zone. We should get away for spring break, just the Three *E*s. Somewhere far from this city and all its guys."

As a way to get my boyfriend and the boy I used to love back on track, I'm at Simon and Mark's apartment preparing a vegetarian meal of sesame noodles in peanut sauce, a new favorite of mine. Simon has run out to get some sparkling water because Mark's contribution to our dinner is a six-pack of beer, and he's already on his second as I put the finishing touches on the noodles. I ask about his police cadet.

"Oh, he's really nice and everything, but we didn't really connect."

"Connect as in he's not your spiritual partner in life's journey, or connect as in you didn't have sex."

He laughs and says, "He's not my spiritual partner."

"So the search continues."

"Yeppers."

Simon enters now with a big bottle of water in each hand. As he puts them on the floor (still no table at the apartment, so we eat picnic-style, with cockroaches substituting for ants), he says, "Smells good," without any real enthusiasm. The atmosphere in this place has been awkward since I first stepped through the doorway. I think in addition to UV warnings, forecasters should also provide Socially Awkward Warnings. You know, the forecaster could say, "A big socially awkward front is headed for Washington Heights. Residents are cautioned to stay indoors and avoid contact with other people, if at all possible."

We sit cross-legged and slurp our noodles as I try to make small talk. Simon is already stressed about midterms while Mark — believe it or not — seems to be homesick for Minnesota. He says, "I miss nature, Moll. All this traffic and congestion and no green space. I miss the woods and the river."

I use this as my opening: "Why don't you go back and visit? I know your parents would love to see you."

But Mark doesn't even respond to the suggestion, just stuffs his face with noodles to avoid saying anything. Simon notices, and surprises me by offering an olive branch, saying, "You could go camping in Maine. That's where my family always went when I was a kid."

This gets Mark's attention. "Yeah, but I've got no gear out here and no car to get to Maine."

"You can tag along with me, if you want. I'm going to spend spring break in the woods. I need to get away."

Mark says, "Really? You wouldn't mind?"

Simon shakes his head. "Not at all."

To me, Mark says, "You in, Moll?"

"Sorry. I'm spending spring break with Lily and Jessie."

Simon asks, "Where are you going?"

I frown. "They still haven't told me yet."

While I'm pleased that Simon has made a peace offering, I'm concerned that out in the wilderness, alone and away from civilization, these two might kill each other. Mark's face tells me he shares my doubts, but the prospect of getting out of the city overrules any reservations he has. He just says, "Cool, I'm in."

I still think it's a bad idea, but the socially awkward front dissipates as the guys go over the preparations they will need to make for a week out in the woods. It's like Mark has become straight and Simon approves. Yes, that's stereotyping on my part. But still, it's a beginning.

All of us survive midterms, although there's a long part of the final stretch in which Simon goes underground, communicationwise, and I have to rely on the other *E*s for motivation, commiseration, and caffeine. Our reward is the weeklong recovery period they call *spring break.* I see Simon and Mark off as they leave the city for the Maine woods. Simon gives me a long kiss good-bye, and part of me regrets not going with them. But Lily and Jessie have committed me to their boy-free spring break.

Other college students go to Florida for spring break. Some of the black students on campus are headed to Atlanta for "Freaknik," the black spring break. Personally, I wanted to just stay in New York and explore the museums, since I don't have the money for a round-trip ticket back to Minnesota. But Lily and Jessie have other plans for me.

So where are the Three *E*s headed?

North.

Lily has always wanted to go to Martha's Vineyard, an island off the coast of Massachusetts, a wealthy resort town that's not too pricey when it's not summer. She's found a small place to rent that's right on the water. First, though, we'll head to Boston, a city none of us has ever seen before, for a night on the town. We're taking the Happy Star bus from Chinatown in Lower Manhattan to Boston, and from Boston Jessie is renting us a car for our time on Martha's Vineyard. When I told Mom about it she said it sounded very romantic and swank, but she's never taken the Happy Star (fifteen dollars one-way to Boston), which, I must say, is not particularly swank *or* romantic.

But it's within my budget, and I wouldn't let Lily pay for a train ticket for me since she was already springing for the rental. I told them I would be perfectly fine meeting them at the Boston train station, but they both insisted on taking the Happy Star with me, saying it would be an adventure.

And an adventure it is. In the back rows, some guys are drinking beer and singing in Spanish. You have to go past them to get to the bathroom, which is a challenge in itself. I don't care what anyone says, peeing on a bus speeding down the highway at over sixty miles per hour is not easy, especially when guys are serenading you on the other side of the door. Add to that, there's no sink for washing your hands.

When I'm done I rush past the singing Spaniards and back to Lily and Jessie, who sit across the aisle from me. In front of them are other college students heading home to Boston for the break; in back of them are two elderly Chinese women arguing loudly.

Lily stares straight ahead, a dead look in her eyes. She says, "Next time I offer to buy you a train ticket, you will simply say 'thank you.'"

Jessie says, "I wonder if I can hold it in till we get to Boston."

Maybe they want me to feel guilty for insisting on the bus, but secretly I'm a little pleased that they're getting to see how the other ninety percent live.

When we arrive at the bus station, Lily and Jessie

heave sighs of relief, and we take the T to our hotel, not far from the Boston Commons. It's a gray, overcast afternoon as we walk down Tremont Street, past the panhandlers and a few tattooed Emerson students all decked out in black and chain-smoking in front of a residence hall. We're in what's called the Theater District, and the marquees we pass advertise musicals and dramas and student productions. Traffic is as thick as the accents, and when we make it to our hotel room, Lily collapses on the bed, saying, "I'm beat."

Jessie is adamant: "Hey, no slacking. We only have one night to see Boston. I've got it all planned out."

Lily groans, "I just need ten minutes."

Jessie says, "Make them ten New York minutes, sistuh-woman-sistuh. We have a lot to see and not much time to see it."

Lily says, "I never realized you were such a tourist."

She pulls a camera out of her backpack and says, "Like Mark, I've decided to come out of the closet." I shoot her a look and she says, "Sorry, Moll. Now, smile, Miss Lily!"

She snaps a photo and turns the lens on me now, saying, "Come on, Molly, say *Le Sueur Peas*!"

I smile, relieved that one of them has turned out to be as big a tourist as I am. After Jessie takes her photo, I whip out my disposable camera that Mark gave (stole for) me and tell Jessie and Lily to pose together. Jessie makes devil's horns behind Lily's head, not realizing Lily's doing the same thing to her.

In less than five hours we see the *Make Way for Ducklings* statues in the Commons, walk the streets of Beacon Hill, visit Mother Goose's grave, tour Paul Revere's house, pretend to pray at the Old North Church, eat an Italian dinner in the North End (where, to Jessie's disappointment, we are carded), stop for dessert at the Modern Bakery, and hail a cab back to the hotel where we make ourselves up for a night at a trendy South End club Jessie has heard about from a friend at Harvard. Lily and I are exhausted, but Jessie can't wait to check out the Boston boys. She loves their accents and says she wouldn't mind meeting a ruddy Irish bartender or a dark Italian pizza-spinner.

Lily says, "Setting aside your ethnic sensitivity for just a moment, I thought we agreed this week would be a boy-free zone."

Jessie says, "Boyfriend-free. A little flirting never hurt anyone."

Serious now, Lily says, "You are *not* bringing a guy back to our hotel room."

Jessie says, "Of course not! Jeez, Lil."

I can't help myself; I say, "I wonder how Simon and Mark are doing."

Lily says, "So call them."

"No reception," I tell her.

Lily says, "I'm sure they're having a grand old time being rugged hunter-slash-gatherers in the deep woods. And the beauty part is that there's no girls around to tempt Simon."

Jessie adds, "And only Simon to tempt Mark, not that . . ." and then she trails off, and suddenly becomes fascinated by the room service menu on the nightstand.

I say, icily, "Not that *what*?"

Jessie squeaks, "Nothing."

"You were going to say, 'not that Simon is tempting,' weren't you?"

Jessie backpedals. "All I meant was that Simon isn't Mark's type. I mean, Mark goes for buff pretty boys . . . and Simon is more . . . the cute, intellectual type."

I sigh.

Lily says, "Boy-free zone."

Jessie says, "We can't even *talk* about guys?"

Lily rolls her eyes. "Fine. New rule. We can only talk about celebrity guys we'll never meet."

Jessie amends Lily's rule, adding, "Or fictional guys. Like Legolas, the world's hottest elf."

I'm still annoyed at Jessie for her comment about Simon, but I let it go and put on my smoky-colored makeup for our night on the town.

The club that Jessie leads us to used to be a fire-house, and, true to form, she somehow gets us in without being carded. A fireman's pole still connects the second floor to the first, but a bouncer keeps the drunk guys from trying to slide down it and the drunk girls from trying to pole dance on it. The music is loud and the dance floor is dark, *really* dark, like we're all just shadows moving to the beat.

Even with visibility this low, guys still hit on Lily and Jessie, so as they dance with Boston boys, I lean against a wall nursing a lite beer, wondering how soon we can leave. I miss Simon, and as I look around, I'm grateful that I'm not in the dating pool, the humiliating, soul-sucking, spirit-crushing, self-esteem-killing dating pool.

And that's when I feel someone tapping me on the shoulder. I turn, and there's a guy a good foot taller than me, wearing a Red Sox T-shirt and jeans. He leans down, shouts in my ear, "How ya doin' tonight?"

Even in this dim light I can make out his features, which are . . . well . . . *beautiful.* I say, "Good." Then I add, "Yeah, I'm doing good."

He says, in a thick Boston accent, "Wow, you gottah helluvah accent going there. Where you from?"

I look at my feet briefly before I tell him, "Minnesota."

He smiles, and his teeth, like his dark eyes and short brown hair, are perfect. Dimples form on his magnificent cheekbones and I think of the old expression *dreamboat,* because that's what he is, and he sailed to me, Molly Swain.

Dreamboat says, "I'm Martin, but everybody calls me Marty."

Another *E* name. Is this a probability wave or, as others would call it, fate? I say, "Molly."

He asks, in his wonderfully rich accent, his dark eyes twinkling, "You wannah dance?"

And I hear my response: "I'd love to."

He takes my hand and leads me to the floor, where we stake out a small space among the dancers who move wildly, fueled by alcohol or loneliness or maybe just plain old lust. Marty catches the eyes of many of the girls and a few of the guys as he dances smoothly, and I imitate his steps, hoping Lily and Jessie spot us together, which they do. Jessie fans her crotch to let me know that Marty is hot, while Lily looks at me with what I would call disapproval.

She's probably just mad Marty didn't ask *her* to dance.

And then it hits me. Am I cheating on Simon?

It's just a dance, after all.

I mean, I haven't kissed him.

The bass line is still pounding when Marty leans down and asks, "I'm gonna get a drink. What can I get you?"

I blush and say, "A lite beer."

"Be right back," he says, and then he gives me a little squeeze.

As Marty heads to the bar, Lily and Jessie dump their guys to surround me. Jessie asks, "Who's *he?*"

"Marty."

Lily says, "You two seem to be hitting it off."

I wipe some sweat from my forehead. "It's just an innocent dance."

Jessie says, "From the way you were looking at him, I'd say there's nothing innocent about it. You shouldn't undress him with your eyes like that. Show him a little respect." Then she laughs.

I defend myself. "I wasn't looking at him that way! We were just dancing."

Marty joins us now and hands me a beer. He says to the other two *Es*, "Hey, how yah doin'?"

Lily politely says that she's fine, but Jessie has to go and say, "Could you be any cuter?"

Marty just smiles and my heart races.

This is so shallow. Just because he's handsome, I'm acting like an idiot. Marty puts an arm around my shoulder and I nearly drop my beer. He kisses the top of my head and says, "I just look good 'cause I'm standin' next to Molly, here."

Be still, my beating heart.

I mean that literally. I think I'm about to go into pulmonary shock.

Lily asks him about himself and we learn that Marty works for his father, a plumber, and that one day he'll take over the family business. Then he says his friends left the club early but he stayed so he could meet me.

"Well, our Molly is something special," Lily says.

Marty says, "I can't believe she doesn't have a boyfriend already."

Jessie says, "I can't believe it, either."

Lily adds, "It's unbelievable."

I grab Marty's drink and hand it and my beer to Lily, saying "Hang on to these." Then I tell Marty, "Let's dance."

We dance and we dance and we dance, and before I know it, Lily and Jessie join us on the floor, saying they're ready to leave.

"You want to go already?" I ask them.

Lily says, "It's almost two. Come on, we have a big day tomorrow."

Marty says, "I can take Molly home."

Jessie and Lily shoot me looks, and as much as it kills me to say it, I say it anyway: "That's okay. I really should go."

Marty looks disappointed, but then he rebounds, pulling my face up to his so he can kiss me.

It's amazing.

It is soooo amazing. The way his tongue moves over mine, the feel of his hands on my cheeks.

I hear Jessie say to Lily, "Go to the bar and order a bucket of cold water."

Marty pulls away, saying, "Thanks for hanging with me tonight, Molly. If you're ever in Boston . . ."

Jessie says, "Kiss *me* like that and I'll transfer here."

On the walk back to the hotel, Lily finally says what I've been waiting for her to say since we left the club. "Glad Simon wasn't here to see that."

Jessie says, "Oh, let her enjoy herself. Jeez, we're on break, you know. What Simon doesn't know can't hurt him."

But now that the thrill has faded, I slink guiltily down the sidewalk. I say, "I shouldn't have kissed him."

Jessie tells me, "It's not a big deal."

"I shouldn't have danced with him."

Jessie repeats, "It's no big deal."

But it is a big deal. The thought that I could do something like that when I have Simon — sweet, trusting Simon — kills me.

We're up another two hours as I confess to every crime ever committed, and Lily and Jessie try to assure me that since nothing happened, there's no harm, no foul. But I lie awake thinking of the look on Simon's face if he ever found out.

We change our plans and stop off at the Lizzie Borden Bed & Breakfast, having a fun, if strange, night, and then head to Martha's Vineyard. Lizzie's bobble head is proudly displayed on the car's dashboard, and the Three *E*s have decided that it will be our trip mascot. Liz-ee is now our honorary fourth *E*.

On the ferry ride to Martha's Vineyard, we position ourselves on the outdoor deck, wrapped in coats and sipping the hot coffee we bought on shore. As I look out on the waves, I tell Lily, "I'm so ashamed of myself."

Lily and Jessie shake their heads. Lily says, "Will you stop beating yourself up? Nothing happened. You were just flattered, is all. It makes you do stupid things."

I make a decision. "I'm going to tell Simon."

At once, they both shout, "No!"

"I don't want to keep secrets from him. It's not healthy for our relationship."

Jessie says, "It was nothing! You want to hurt him, go on. Tell him you had a couple beers and then made out with this really hot guy in Boston."

Lily agrees. "It was just a slip on your part. Don't make Simon suffer for it. You've learned your lesson, so move on."

"I don't know," I mumble.

Lily puts an arm around me, saying, "Forgive yourself. And do Simon a favor: Keep it to yourself. Unless . . ."

"Unless what?"

Lily says, "Unless what you're really trying to do is break up with Simon."

I think of Simon's crooked lips and ears that stick out a little too far, and I say, "No. God, no."

Our cabin is not far from the Aquinnah Lighthouse, a short walk to a beautiful, sandy, rocky beach with dunes that are perfect for lying on as you gaze up at the sky to watch the clouds roll by. We spend the days walking the shoreline collecting shells and stones or driving into the small towns for meals and shopping. I, for example, have bought T-shirts for Simon, Mark, Mom, Dad (XXX-large just in case he's still binging on junk food when he's on the road), and, yes, even Russ, my non-virginal brother. Since we indulged Jessie in her guilty pleasure (the Lizzie Borden house), today we're visiting the beach that — as Lily has informed us — is where they shot the "panicked crowd" scene in *Jaws.*

On the ride out, Jessie says, "I thought you only liked art films."

Lily says, "I'm not a film snob. Well, not too big of a film snob, anyway." She has her camera with her, so we can take pictures of her running and screaming on the beach. She has an old T-shirt in her bag that she marked up with lipstick so it looks like blood. A sleeve's cuff is drenched in red.

I say, "You *both* have your morbid sides."

Lily says, "*Jaws* is a classic."

Jessie says, "Lizzie is history," as she pats the bobble head.

Lily says, "Come on, Molly, what horrible, gruesome thing fascinates you?"

I tell her honestly that I don't know.

When we arrive at the beach, Lily changes into her bloody T-shirt and rolls up her pant legs. She wades in the cold ocean water as she positions Jessie about twenty feet in front of her for a head-on shot, while I'm standing just at the water's edge for a side shot. Lily splashes some water on her face and hair, saying, "Remember — I want you to capture the look of terror on my face."

Jessie says, "Okay, film know-it-all. What, as they say, is your motivation?"

Lily says, "I just had a shark take a bite out of me. Duh." She pulls her arm into her red sleeve and puts it behind her back so it looks like it's been bitten off.

Jessie says, affecting a haughty director's tone, "No, no, no. I don't want a re-creation here. I want genuine personal terror. I want you to reach deep inside yourself and confront that one thing that frightens you the most. Can you? Can you face your worst fear, damn you!"

Lily says, "My worst fear? Let me think." She pauses in the ocean, mulling it over. Suddenly, she looks up, says, "Got it!" before she runs screaming out of the water, a look of sheer terror on her face.

Once we've snapped her picture, I ask her, "So what was your motivation?"

She says, "Spending the rest of my life with Nathan because I didn't want to hurt his feelings. Your turn."

I take off my shoes and socks and step into the Atlantic, which is colder than I had imagined. Jessie aims her camera at me, asking, "Motivation?"

I say, "It's October, Mark just told me he's gay, and on top of that he thinks I'm a lesbian."

Lily says, "And . . . action!"

I run screaming out of the water but I'm laughing so hard I fall down in the sand.

When it's Jessie's turn, she tells us her motivation is "having to take Lit Hum again." Then she runs out of the water with a bloodcurdling cry worthy of every slasher film ever made.

Lily says, excited, "Oh, wait, do me again!"

She runs into the water as I shout, "What's your motivation?"

She shouts back, "My supermarket back home stops making their Farmer Jack brand French onion dip!" And then she lets out cries like a banshee as she propels herself ashore, falling down, crawling through the sand, dramatically moaning, "My . . . God. My god has . . . forsaken me."

I frame her face, wet and sandy, as I silently give thanks for my friends. It's wonderful to know that these are the good old days as you live them, not recognizing them only in hindsight.

The three of us take the train back to New York (Lily insists). When we arrive at JJ, we look at each other sadly, mourning the end of our week together on a beautiful island off the Massachusetts coast. Why can't life be like that all the time? We hug one another before we return to our rooms, sighing at the prospect of classes. At least I have the Brian Greene guest lecture to look forward to.

There are messages waiting for me: Mom wants to know about Boston and Martha's Vineyard, Dad's called from a truck stop in Wisconsin to make sure I made it back to JJ safely, and Mark has left a message saying that we need to talk.

Whenever someone says *We need to talk*, you know it's not about anything good. When I call back, Mark sounds distant, and we make plans to meet the next day.

After my last class of the day I find Mark in the lobby of JJ, sitting at the grand piano, wondering, no doubt, if visitors are allowed to play it. He pantomimes playing, his fingers never quite touching the keys.

When he finally notices me standing next to him, he stops abruptly, embarrassed.

I say, "I didn't know you could play."

He admits, "I can't. I just like to pretend." Then he adds, "You're late. They called up to your room, but you weren't there."

I look at my watch. "I'm not even five minutes late. So what's wrong? You're acting all weird on me."

He stands up now, looking at me uncertainly. "It's just . . . nothing. This was a bad idea."

I look at him — tall, skinny Mark, whose sleepy eyes are open wide right now. "What's wrong? Is it your parents?"

"I haven't talked to my parents." He thinks about

something for a moment, and then he looks at me carefully. Finally, he says, "Let's go to your room. We really need to talk."

Oh great, it's something *I* did. What did I do? I didn't do anything. Did I?

In the elevator I try to pry it out of him, but he insists on waiting. Once we're in my room he closes the door behind us and locks it. He points to the bed and tells me to have a seat. He sits on the desk, his arms folded across his chest, his head down as if he's ashamed of me. I remind myself that there is no way he could know about Marty.

Now I'm *really* nervous. I ask, "What's wrong?"

Without looking at me, he says softly, "You know, Moll, you're the best friend I've ever had. You helped me graduate and you didn't freak when you found out I was gay."

I take in a deep breath. "What did I do?"

Now he looks up at me, a sad smile on his beautiful face. He says, "Nothing. Moll, nothing at all. Do you think I'm mad at you?"

"I don't know what to think. You're freaking me out."

He shifts a little, nervous. He says, "I wish I didn't have to tell you this, but I don't think I've gotta choice here. Moll. Simon . . ." But then he doesn't say anything else.

I feel my heart beating. "You're scaring me. Is he all right?"

"He's fine. I mean, there's nothing wrong with him. I mean, he's healthy."

"What are you talking about?"

His voice cracks as he says, "Simon's in love with me."

"Very funny. Are you in some sort of trouble?"

He looks at me, astounded. "No! Jesus, Molly, I'm serious! Simon came out to me. He said he loves me."

I feel numb. "What?"

He takes a deep breath before he says, "He's been weird for weeks. When I moved in, it was like he didn't approve of me because I'm gay, but for months it's like he's been flirting with me. Stealing glances, making comments — that kind of thing. I thought I was imagining it. But then when we went camping, he just broke down and told me. He's been in love with me ever since we spent New Year's Eve together in Times Square."

I look at my feet as I whisper, "Why are you doing this to me?"

"I'm so sorry, Moll. I wish it wasn't true. I swear to God, I thought I was just imagining it at first. I didn't want this to happen. I told him that there could never be anything between us — I don't feel that way about him. And I could never do something like that to you."

There's a concept in physics called *singularity*. Simply stated, it is where a devastating rupture occurs in the fabric of space and time.

Singularity.

It's almost funny, if you think about it. A devastating rupture is just another way of saying *alone*.

Mark asks, "Moll, are you okay?"

I nearly laugh, but instead I start to cry. I just look at him: beautiful Mark Dahl, who is so out of my league. Mark Dahl, the first boy I ever fell in love with. The poor little farm boy with a secret. The guy I just can't do enough for.

I hate him.

I think I hear him say, "Moll?"

I wipe my eyes; I don't want to appear hysterical. I try to keep my voice even; I try to stay in control. "You just couldn't stand to see me happy, could you? What did you do, Mark, get him drunk?"

"Molly, I didn't —"

"What did I ever do to you but be nice? And this is how you pay me back? Jesus, Mark, all you ever do is think of yourself! I mean, Jesus! You know how much Simon means to me, and just because you get horny, you try it with him?"

"Molly, I swear —"

"He's so . . . innocent. He's never even had sex! We were *waiting*, Mark, *waiting*! Jesus, how could you do this? How could you do this to me?"

Mark stands now and, hugging himself, says in a faint voice, "Moll . . . I'm so sorry."

And now I can't help it, I just start crying harder. "This is why Simon didn't call me when he got back. He can't face me. All because of you!" I stand up now, right in front of him. I stand straight with my shoulders back because I am NOT that weak little nobody anymore; maybe I never really was.

I'm the daughter-of-a-bastard truck driver from the Valley of the fucking Green Giant, and I'm not gonna take it anymore. I yell, "Get the hell out of my room and stay the hell out of my life!"

There's this look on his face — the distant, hurt look, the one that, like an idiot, I fell in love with on Valentine's Day over a year ago. He says, so quietly that I'm not even sure I've heard him right, "Okay. I will, Moll. I'll go away."

❖ ❖ ❖

Mark leaves the door open, and now Lily is peeking her head in, concerned. She says, "What's wrong?"

I can't say anything.

Lily sits next to me on the bed and pets my hair. She says, "Honey, what's wrong?"

So I just tell her. "Mark said that Simon's in love with him."

Lily says, "That isn't funny."

I say, "You think I'm *trying* to be funny?" Then I just sit there, crying.

Next, Jessie appears, wants to know what's wrong. Lily says, "Mark told her that Simon's in love with him."

Jessie says, "What?"

Lily says, "It's true."

I manage to say, in between breaths, "Simon is *not* in love with Mark. He's in love with *me*."

Jessie sits on the bed now, too. Even if I wanted to get up, I can't — Jessie and Lily both have their arms around me. Jessie whispers, "Why would Mark say something like that if it wasn't true?"

"Because," I sniffle, "he's just ashamed of himself. He couldn't tell his parents he was gay. He couldn't tell me that he made a pass at Simon."

Lily says, "That doesn't sound like Mark."

Of course, no one showed up for dinner at the Cuban restaurant, but everyone's schedule is free for my breakdown. Maybe-Chris arrives next. He says to Jessie, "*There* you are." And now he says, "What's wrong?"

Jessie says, "It's complicated."

Maybe-Chris says, "Oh." Then Maybe-Chris says, "Come on, Jess, let's leave them alone."

Jessie says, "No, I have to stay here."

Maybe-Chris tells her, "But we have plans . . . you know."

Jessie says, "Why don't you make your plans by yourself? How would that be?"

Maybe-Chris says, "Typical, that's how it would be." Before he leaves, Maybe-Chris says, "Hope you feel better, Molly."

Jessie closes the door, and then, like I'm still the corpse at a wake, Lily and Jessie whisper to each other.

Jessie: "I hate to say this, but I thought Simon had a thing for Mark."

Lily: "Why? I didn't pick up on anything."

Jessie: "I'm sorry, that night we went out skating? Simon kept sneaking peeks at Mark. And he kept scowling at the gay guys who were there. Jeez, that's two guys Molly's fallen for who've come out of the closet."

I finally speak. "Simon is *not* gay!"

A chorus now of *sorry*s and *oh, honey*s, and *we love you*s echo against the walls in my tiny room. I manage to untangle myself from Jessie and Lily, get up, and walk to the door, which I open wide. I say, "I need to be alone."

Now a chorus of *but*s and *are you sure?*s.

They finally agree and leave slowly, offering whatever I need — a late-night talk, a dinner out, a bottle of wine — to help me through this. When they're out the door, I close it, lean against it, and stare at the pile of books on my desk that are waiting for me to read them regardless of whatever else is going on in my life.

But they will have to wait.

I wipe my face with a towel, put on a coat, and grab a cab I can't really afford and give the driver Simon's address in Washington Heights.

He doesn't come down to let me in on the first buzz or the second, but by the third he's standing on the other side of the door. Through the iron bars of the window-pane he looks lost, like a little boy who wandered away from his parents at the park. When he opens the door, he hugs me and whispers, "Molly."

I hug him back, but his body's rigid, he won't relax in my arms. I say, "Mark came to see me."

He holds me at arm's length, looks into my face. He asks urgently, "What did he say?"

I just say, "Come on, let's go upstairs. We need to talk."

Once we're in his apartment — and once he's sat me down next to him on the couch that he and Mark rescued from a curb — he takes my hand in his. Calmly, evenly, he says, "What did Mark tell you?"

So I just say it: "He told me that you're in love with him."

Simon stands up now and paces back and forth. "Jesus! I knew it! I knew he'd try to make it seem like it was all my fault!"

I just sit there, dazed. I say, "Make *what* seem like your fault?"

He looks at me, red, furious. He says, "We had a few beers . . . and when I was drunk . . . he made a pass at me."

"He made a pass at you?"

He spits out, "Yeah! And I was so out of it I didn't realize what was happening at first."

I just sit on the couch, like something dead that's been washed up onshore. I ask, "Where is he?"

Simon runs a hand through his hair, says, "Oh, he's outta here. As soon as we got back from Maine, he left. Good riddance."

I can't think of anything to say, so I repeat myself. "He said you were in love with him."

He leans down now, puts his hand on my cheek. He says, "Molly, I'm in love with *you*."

I think about how long I've wanted him to say that to me. I had pictured candlelit dinners, flowers, maybe even going all the way.

He straightens back up, says, "I never should have let him move in with me. But you were so insistent. I never should have done it."

I say, "I didn't think anything like this would happen!"

He grunts, saying, "I can't believe he would do this. I just can't fucking believe it."

"Neither can I," I whisper.

He mutters, "Some friend. Why didn't you just come out and tell me that you were in love with him once?"

I look up at him, at his crooked lips that look like they've just tasted poison, at his ears that stick out like radars, just waiting for a storm. I say, "I'm sorry."

He says, "I guess you just thought I was the best you

could do, huh? You couldn't have Mark, so I was the consolation prize. You know, it was all I could do to ask you out. When you've been rejected your whole life, it's pure hell to put yourself out there. But I did. For you."

I think about Boston, about Marty, and I feel like the most selfish person who ever lived. I say, "I'm sorry."

He takes in a deep breath now and exhales it slowly. "I introduced you to my parents. They really like you. I thought we had a good thing. I thought it was worth waiting for. And then Mark grabs my dick and tells you I love him, and this is what I get. I mean, Jesus, Molly."

All I can think to say is, "I'm sorry." And then I start to cry. Because I was in love with Mark. Because I was the one who asked Simon to share his place with him. Because I kissed a guy in Boston just because he was handsome.

Simon sits down next to me. He puts his arm around me as he says, "I'm sorry for losing my temper. Molly, I love *you*."

I wipe my eyes, say, "I love you, too."

He kisses the top of my head before he says, "I love you, Molly."

And in spite of the fact it's what I've been waiting to hear, I just can't quite make myself believe it.

❖ ❖ ❖

The days pass me by in a daze. Simon is devoted: He calls, he comes by every Wednesday and spends the night, holding me in his arms, which I can't seem to get enough of. Lily and Jessie are worried: They check in on me, try to draw me out, but I tell them that everything's fine, that Simon and I are better than ever, that Simon loves me and I love him. They've stopped offering an opinion on the subject, maybe thinking that my kiss with Marty was proof that I had my own doubts. Maybe they just can't understand how Simon and I are together when Lily broke it off with Nathan and Jessie can't seem to make it work with Maybe-Chris.

I don't even know why I'm here, but here I am. Outside the Times Square Duane Reade where Mark works, where he shoplifted gifts for me. I look out at the traffic, the long lines of yellow cabs and buses and cars. I watch the people walk down the street, some rude, refusing to get out of anyone's way, others seemingly in another world as they talk on their cell phones. And then there are the tourists and lovers, the people who walk hand in hand, putting their confidence on display for the whole world to see. As I watch them, the couples, I wonder what challenges they've faced, what secrets they've kept from each other. I wonder how they found each other. I wonder when they decided they were in love, how they told each other the news.

I enter the store and make my way like a spy to an aisle where I can see the cashiers, where I can easily duck out of view. He's there, grimly scanning the items shoppers bring him, bagging them, telling customers, in a monotone voice, to *have a good day.*

That's what we tell one another in Minnesota. To have a good day. Most New Yorkers don't say that. Maybe they think it's superficial or clichéd. Or maybe they just don't care if you have a good day or not.

I wonder why Mark hasn't called to let me know where he's staying. But then, I was the one who told him to get out of my life.

He seems okay to me — not good, but okay. In spite of myself, I still want to talk to him, rid him of his guilty conscience, make him come clean. But I can't make myself do it.

I take the subway back to campus, staring blankly like the other passengers, and when I get to JJ, Simon is there in the lobby, waiting for me, his face deep in concentration over his laptop. He doesn't notice me from where I stand behind him. When I say, "Hi," he smiles and stands up to give me a hug. He says, "Hey, Molly."

I stand there, in his embrace, trying to take its measure, judge its sincerity. But it feels so good, and, truth be told, for right now that's enough. Just his arms around me is enough.

APRIL

At last, the day has arrived. Lily and Jessie keep shooting me concerned looks, Simon still refuses to discuss Mark, and Mark himself hasn't called or e-mailed or stopped by since it all happened.

But I can't let these things bother me now.

This is why I'm in New York. This is why I enrolled at Columbia. This is the man who made me a budding string theorist. I settle in my chair, waiting for the moment when the professor announces his name. Yes, some girls are obsessed with rockers, others with actors.

Me? It begins and ends with physicists.

And suddenly there he is: Brian Greene, string theorist, M theorist, the man I admire most on this planet. The man whose footsteps I want to follow in. My inspiration.

You can tell we have a celebrity in our midst. The class stands with me to give him an opening ovation. When we finally sit, he begins his lecture, which I listen to in a blur. I can't seem to take notes. I just can't believe it. I see him, I hear him, and yet, I just can't believe it. Only one thing he says sticks in my brain: that during the last hundred years, discoveries in physics have suggested revisions to our everyday sense of reality that are as dramatic, as mind-bending, and as paradigm-shaking as the most imaginative science fiction.

And before I realize what's happened, it's time for questions. The first one is why he finds physics so exciting.

He looks out at the class and says, "Well, the thing that excites me about physics is that it really seeks to answer some of the deepest questions about the physical universe."

Yes! This man understands what's important.

The next question is about any other area of science that fascinates him.

He says, "The science of the mind. What is consciousness? Does it have a physical basis that we can describe by understanding the circuitry of the brain? I think those are some of the deepest questions about life, and outside of physics, I'd say those for me are the most absorbing questions."

The deepest questions about life. I think about that, and suddenly I'm having a moment of crystal clarity, as if my own brain's circuitry, unimpeded by what I want, has calculated an answer to the question that I didn't want to admit had been plaguing me.

I try to be a scientific observer. I look at the data. I remember how Simon always picked me up in my room when Mark was my squatter. I remember that Simon agreed to have Mark be his roommate when he didn't even really know him, just what he looked like. I remember the ugly looks Simon shot the gay police rookie who was flirting with Mark at the roller disco. I remember that it was Simon who invited Mark to spend a week in the wilderness with him. I remember that night I wanted to go all the way, and Simon and I agreed to wait. I remember the looks Simon would give Mark, which I always thought were about me.

I've sought my answer, and now here it is.

I realize that Mark is telling the truth.

And that I just couldn't bear to hear it.

Simon usually shows up in my room every Wednesday, around four or five o'clock. It's become something of a routine that we study, get something to eat, study some more, and then, sometimes, he spends the night. We used to fall asleep on my bed with our arms around each other, but lately he's been complaining that it's hard to get a good night's sleep cramped on my single bed.

It was never a problem for me. I'm going to miss it.

When Simon shows up at my dorm room as usual, he's agitated. He's behind on this studies, he's worried that he can't afford the apartment by himself. He mumbles, cursing Mark's irresponsibility, just moving out like that without a word. The embrace he gives me is perfunctory, but when he pulls away, he understands, without a single word, that things have changed.

He asks, a frustrated look in his eyes, "What's wrong?"

Do I really want to do this now? But if not now, when? So I just say it.

"I wish you had been honest with me."

He shakes his head, angry. "About what?"

"Everything. We could have still been friends, Simon. You could have told me you were gay."

He looks at me, stunned. "I can't believe we're going over this again. Why are you taking his side?"

"I've spent the last few hours thinking about it, and thinking about it, and I can't come up with one single reason why Mark would lie to me."

"You just love Mark Dahl, like you always have and

you always will. *Everybody* loves Mark." He points at my desk, where I still have Mark's high school graduation picture displayed. In spite of everything that's happened, I couldn't get rid of it.

I look into Simon's eyes, his hurt, confused eyes, and I say, "I'm not in love with Mark, not anymore. It was a stupid crush. And there was no reason for it. It's not like he ever led me on."

Simon mutters, "And you think that *I* led you on?"

I try not to cry when I ask, "Didn't you? You told me you loved me. What would you call it?"

His eyes mist now, and he says bitterly, "Maybe I just said it because you were so desperate to hear it. Pleasing other people. That's my job, isn't it?"

I fold my arms across my chest and look at my feet, in their dingy white socks and beat-up sneakers. Then I get angry. Hurt angry. I tell him, "I don't understand why you're having such a hard time admitting to yourself who you really are. And I don't understand why you had to drag *me* into it. This is Manhattan, not some small town. It's the twenty-first century. I honestly don't understand." My voice cracks as I say, "Didn't you know that I would fall in love with you? Didn't I count at all?"

Simon says, "I am *not* doing this again. You always

take his side. Guess what, Molly, he's not going to fall in love with you, no matter what you do!" He looks at me, heartbroken. I recognize the look; it's the one I wore back in October when I found out that Mark was gay. I know what it's like to love Mark and not be loved back. I understand that look, even if he won't admit it. But I also understand, like I've understood nothing else in my life before, that it's not my problem. And yet, I still want to feel Simon's arms around me, I want him to tell me that he loves me. I still want what I can't have.

There are just some things you simply can't change, no matter how much you want them to. So I hear myself say, "Good-bye, Simon."

He says nothing. He just leaves, slamming the door behind him.

Days go by slowly, like time has dropped dead. Lily and Jessie have told me I did the right thing, but then they always believed Mark and I'm humiliated (yet again) to be the last one to realize that Mark had told the truth. I wonder how I could be so stupid. It's all I can do to get out of bed in the morning. I try to read, but nothing sticks. I attend lectures, but I can't bring myself to write down one damn thing. I second-guess myself, I wonder what I did wrong. I wonder if this is all my fault, if I turn them gay. And I ask myself if I really loved Simon when I kissed another guy behind his back.

I'm all self-doubt and shame, wrapped up in jeans that are too big for me.

Simon doesn't call, but his mother does, and she's anxious to get together so the two of us *kids* (Simon and I) *can get back on track.* She's left so many messages that I finally decide to pick up halfway through her latest and agree to meet for dinner tonight. Obviously, no one has let her in on the news that when Simon was making out with me he was pretending I was Mark.

The Three *E*s gather at Café 212, and I skip my makeup and lipstick, preferring to wear shame and humiliation, along with a black fleece pullover and the too-big jeans.

Lily and Jessie notice my new old look but decide not to comment. Lily has ordered me a triple mocha in the hopes of restarting my pulse, while Jessie presents me with her breakup CD, which she burned last year after her high school boyfriend dumped her for a *cheap hoochie mama.* She says, "It's good for wallowing in self-pity and plotting revenge."

Lily asks, "Have you talked to Mark about this?"

I shake my head. "I stopped by his job again, but I couldn't face him."

Lily looks meaningfully at Jessie and says, "We need a ladies' night out. Just the Three *E*s."

I moan, "Slapping on two coats of makeup and downing martinis isn't going to help anything."

Lily says, "Can't hurt."

Jessie asks, "What are you going to tell Simon's mother?"

I sniff my triple mocha. I say, "I haven't decided yet."

Jessie says, "You should tell her the truth."

Lily says, "Don't do that. I know you're hurt, but she needs to hear this news from the source."

I sniff. "You mean like I did?"

Lily just looks at me and says, "Oh, what a tangled web we weave."

When I arrive at the little café near Washington Square, Simon's mother is already waiting at a table, a glass of white wine in her hand. When she sees me she stands up and gives me a hug, and then she briefly stares at my outfit, my makeup-less face. As we sit down she says, "Forgive me for saying so, but you don't look well."

I say, "I don't feel well, either."

She wastes no time. "Simon won't say a word about what happened between you two. I just don't under-stand — you were getting along so famously."

I have nothing to say to that.

She frowns, concerned. "Let's order." She calls over the waiter and orders a bowl of soup for herself, and I say, "Just coffee." Simon's mother says, "Oh no, you have to eat something. Please."

I say, "I'm not hungry."

She tells the waiter to give me a few minutes to decide. When he's gone, she says, "Whatever he did, I know he's deeply sorry. I hope you're not letting your pride get in the way."

I can't help it, I actually laugh for the first time in days. "*My* pride?"

She looks at me, confused. She says, "Please, tell me what happened. You and Simon aren't speaking to each other. I don't understand. And Simon refuses to talk about it. What did he do? It's just not like him to make people angry. Drive them crazy? Yes. Make them mad? No. I know he's very sorry for whatever it was."

"You should be talking about this with Simon."

"I've tried, Molly. Honestly, I have tried. This seems bigger than a lovers' quarrel to me. Is he pressuring you . . . you know. For sex? Did he get a little too fresh?"

"No. I can tell you truthfully that he is not pressuring me for sex."

"Then I really don't understand."

When I don't say anything, she leans in, says seriously, "Is there anything I can do to get you two back on track? Won't you please tell me what happened, so I can try and fix it? You both seem so miserable right now, it's breaking my heart."

I look at Simon's mother — Simon's sweet, thoughtful, somewhat overbearing mother, who loves the Simon I loved. I couldn't see the obvious, why should I blame her for failing to, too?

I say, "Your son . . ."

Her eyes are fearful.

"Your son and I just want different things."

I think of Mark and realize I just lied without meaning to.

She leans back, relieved and disappointed. She says, "Let me call the waiter back; you really need to eat some food."

❖ ❖ ❖

I've allowed Jessie to make me up for our night on the town, and Lily has bought me a new dress, sleek and black, for which she's probably paid too much. The Three *E*s are outfitted entirely in black as we enter a hot new club on the Upper East Side, which Jessie heard about from Maybe-Chris. We shouldn't even be able to get in, but the Push Room's bouncer now works here and waves us in after Jessie slips him some cash. As it turns out, Maybe-Chris is at the bar with a date, prompting Jessie to order us a round of double apple martinis. When they arrive at our little table in a dark corner of the club, Lily raises her glass to propose a toast. Jessie has to be convinced to raise hers, since she's busy shooting nasty looks at the bar. I don't have the energy to lift mine.

Lily says, "Come on, Molly. Join us."

I pretend I'm doing a bench press and summon all my strength to raise my glass to theirs. Lily says, "To the Three *E*s."

Jessie says, "To us."

I say, "Yeah."

We sip at our drinks and then sit in silence for a moment.

By the second round, I start talking: "You know, I just thought someone had finally fallen for me. Me! Molly Swain. He was my first real boyfriend, you know?"

Jessie says, "We know, honey."

"You two have had boyfriends, I mean real boyfriends. Mine are always hiding behind a closet door."

Lily laughs. "We've had a sighting of the old Molly. Welcome back."

But I'm not quite ready to be funny Molly yet. I say, "It's not fair. Do I do this to myself? Is there some part of me that searches out gay guys because they're safe? Or do I just turn men off women entirely?"

Jessie says, "Don't be ridiculous. The only reason I had my doubts about Simon was the way he sneaked looks at Mark. Otherwise I wouldn't have had a clue."

Lily points out, "The only thing he really seemed passionate about was matrix theory."

"Maybe I'm just a . . . what do you call them, Jessie? Fag hags?"

Lily says, "That term is insulting to both fags and hags."

I ignore her comment. "I saw some at that dance I took Mark to. Fat straight girls who hang out with pretty gay men. Maybe I should just gain a hundred pounds and hang out at gay bars. I can be everyone's big fat best friend."

Lily tries to stop me. "Molly, come on."

"Nothing about Simon led me to believe he was gay," Jessie offers. "And I have excellent gaydar."

A good point, but I'm on a rant. "Maybe I can start a gay dating service," I say. *"Hey, fellas, the guy you like not gay? Introduce him to me, and presto, homo, he's all yours!* I could make a fortune. There'd be a waiting list." Lily and Jessie laugh, and maybe I *am* ready to be funny Molly again, or maybe it's just a reflex.

I don't feel funny, just incredibly bitter.

We finish our second round, order a third. Other topics arise.

"The problem," Jessie tries to say, "is that I really enjoy being with Chris. I mean, when I have him to myself, he's really very good to me. I just wish he would stop seeing other girls."

Lily says, "You can't change someone. I tried to change Nate, and all he did was become more the same."

In the midst of our third round, a group of guys comes by our table. The tallest one, a black man with two gold earrings, says, "And how are you ladies this fine evening?"

I look him in the eyes and say, "Are you gay?"

He looks offended, says, "No!"

"Do you wanna be?" I ask.

He looks at his friends, two shorter white guys wearing tight silk T-shirts, and says, "These bitches are crazy," as he leads them away.

Lily looks at me, concerned. "Molly, don't say stuff like that. You never know how a straight man will react. Some are pretty insecure."

Jessie says, "No insecurities there," as she nods in the direction of Maybe-Chris, who's laughing with a girl who wears a blouse with a neckline that ends somewhere just above the navel.

Lily pushes away her half-empty glass, and says, "I think we've had enough."

Jessie, who's really fuming now as Maybe-Chris leaves the club with the hoochie mama, says, "Or not enough."

So I just blurt out, "Jessie, do you really think Chris is worth a hangover?"

She looks at me and I think that maybe she's in love with the guy. A guy she can't have. I know that feeling better than anyone in this place. This city. This hemisphere. She says, "I suppose not. How about I have a hangover for the hangover's sake?"

Lily says, "You're not *really* in love with Chris, are you?"

She hesitates a moment or two before she says, "It wouldn't make sense."

I grunt, "Does it ever?"

But Lily says to Jessie, "I didn't ask you if it made sense. I asked you if you really are in love with him."

Jessie says, "Yes. Yes, I am. Not a lot. Just a little."

I'm buzzed, so I say, "He can't keep it in his pants."

Jessie shoots me a look before she says, "At least it comes out for the ladies."

Lily says, "That'll do, pigs."

Jessie holds out her hand to me. She says, "Sorry, Moll."

I take it and say, "My fault. Like always."

Now Jessie says, "No, I've been an idiot. He can't change. And I can't make him. I should just cut my losses."

Lily says, "Now that's what I call something to celebrate. Come on, ladies, it's time to hit the floor."

I say, "I don't feel like dancing."

Jessie adds, "Neither do I."

But Lily just grabs us by the wrists and pulls us out on the floor. She screams, "Shake your boo-taay!"

Jessie and I shuffle back and forth.

Lily screams again, "I believe I said, *Shake it!*"

So, to please Lily, Jessie and I put some effort into it, and before you know it, I am close to what one might actually call enjoying myself. And Jessie gives what looks to be a sincere smile and a laugh when Lily slaps her on the ass.

The next song is emblazoned on my memory — it's the song that was playing when the first guy asked Mark to dance at the community center. It was the first song I watched him dance to with another man. I remember it so well because I felt so fat and depressed and mad at myself. But the other thing I remember is how scared-but-happy Mark looked. Every once in a while his eyes would dart over to me as if I were his anchor in a rough sea.

As Jessie dips Lily, I decide I can't put it off anymore. I really have to see Mark.

Okay, so I'm a *little* hungover. I slip out of bed, and slip on a black top and my too-big jeans. The hallway is empty.

I need some fresh air so I head down to the lobby, where the grand piano and the chandelier and the fireplace are bathed in early morning shadow. I step out on 114th Street, barefoot, let the cold sidewalk wake me up. I rub my eyes, my red, bloodshot eyes.

And that's when I hear his voice. He says, "Moll!"

He's dressed in jeans and a long-sleeve shirt, his dark brown hair lifted slightly by the wind, his square jaw pointed in my direction.

He's my first love.

I say, "Hey, Mark."

He walks toward me, stands less than a foot away. He says, "I've thought about calling you."

My immediate impulse is to say, *So why didn't you?* but with him, today, I tell the truth: "I didn't want to talk to you."

He nods. "I get it. I just wanted you to know I didn't, you know, try to get him to like me or anything. And then when he told me he was in love with me, I didn't know how to tell you. I didn't want you to be hurt."

I look up at him, take in his sleepy eyes and thin lips. I say, "Where are you living?"

He says, in his aunt's phlegmy voice, "Back in Montclair, sweetheart. Just until I can afford a place of my own." I can't help it, I laugh. Now Mark says, without a trace of irony, "I would never cheat on you, Molly."

I ask him, "Have you talked to Simon?"

He nods. "Just once. He called me. He's afraid of breaking his parents' hearts."

I shake my head, wondering why gay boys care so much about what their parents think. I say, "I don't know. Your mom seemed to handle it well over Christmas."

He mumbles, "Still early days, yet."

We look at each other for a moment in silence, the only sound the sporadic early morning traffic of Morningside Heights.

I say, "This is called synchronicity. You and me running into each other like this. Just last night I decided that I had to see you."

He smiles. He says, "If synchronicity is me standing outside of JJ for the past week before my shift at Duane Reade — you know, hoping I'd see you, because I was afraid to pick up the phone — well, then, it's synchronicity. If you say so. You're the one with the scholarship to Columbia, after all."

I look up at the sky, at the new day just beginning, and wonder what it will bring. And then I say, "I think I really was in love with him. Not like I was with you . . ." He blushes, but I honestly don't care. I mean, why lie about it? He must have known. Even though I'm the only reason he graduated from high school, he's not stupid. I stretch, my hands behind my head, as I say, ". . . but still, it seemed real. And I liked it. I liked being held in his arms. I liked meeting his parents. I liked being the girlfriend. Call me shallow."

He smiles, says, "You're about as far from shallow as anyone I've met. You know, you were the first person who knew about me. About who I really am. Yeah, I get that it's not what you wanted, but you were still there for me, Moll. You were my friend when I really needed one. And I love you for that."

We look at each other, the street, the sky. He says, "I'm sorry."

It takes me a minute to put my pride, my indignation, and my humiliation aside, before I can say, "I'm the one who owes you an apology. I assumed the worst because . . ." And I take a deep breath, because sometimes in life, you just have to take a deep breath before you tell the truth. ". . . it was easier. It was just easier. I'm so sorry, Mark."

And then this amazing thing happens. He holds out his arms. And I just fall into them. He holds me tight, and I feel so many things — passion, friendship, resentment. But mostly, I feel love.

It feels amazing.

I close my eyes and ask him, like I've always wanted to since I first found out, "Why aren't you straight?"

He laughs just a little before he asks me, "Why aren't you a gay man?"

And we hold each other tighter. Our way of preventing each other from falling down.

He whispers in my ear, "You hungry? How about breakfast? My treat."

I say, "But I need a shower. I mean, my hair. My face."

He just laughs, for the first time in a long time. He says, "You look beautiful, Moll."

I guess you could call this a love story. Not the one I wanted or imagined, but a love story, all the same.